"Miss Martin? Miranda Martin?"

Both Mark and Miranda froze.

"My name is Jack Parsons. I'm an acquaintance of your sister's."

"Lisa?" Miranda felt her heart jump. "Has something happened to her?"

"No, she's okay. She wanted me to give you this." The man held out an envelope. "And I have a delivery for you in my car."

She was looking down at the envelope in her hand, when she heard Mark say in a rather odd voice, "Um, Miranda? I think I know what the delivery is."

She looked up at him, then turned to see what he was staring at so intently. Her own jaw dropped. "Oh, no."

Jack Parsons was on his way back to her, dragging two large, wheeled suitcases behind him. And tagging behind those suitcases like little ducklings were a couple of sandy-haired boys with rumpled clothes and identical faces....

Dear Reader,

Most of us look forward to October for the end-of-the-month treats, but we here at Silhouette Special Edition want you to experience those treats all month long—beginning, this time around, with the next book in our MOST LIKELY TO... series. In *The Pregnancy Project* by Victoria Pade, a woman who's used to getting what she wants, wants a baby. And the man she's earmarked to help her is her arrogant ex-classmate, now a brilliant, if brash, fertility expert.

Popular author Gina Wilkins brings back her acclaimed FAMILY FOUND series with *Adding to the Family,* in which a party girl turned single mother of twins needs help—and her handsome accountant *(accountant?),* a single father himself, is just the one to give it. In *She's Having a Baby,* bestselling author Marie Ferrarella continues her miniseries, THE CAMEO, with this story of a vivacious, single, pregnant woman and her devastatingly handsome—if reserved—next-door neighbor. Special Edition welcomes author Brenda Harlen and her poignant novel *Once and Again,* a heartwarming story of homecoming and second chances. *About the Boy* by Sharon DeVita is the story of a beautiful single mother, a widowed chief of police...and a matchmaking little boy. And Silhouette is thrilled to have *Blindsided* by talented author Leslie LaFoy in our lineup. When a woman who's inherited a hockey team decides that they need the best coach in the business, she applies to a man who thought he'd put his hockey days behind him. But he's been...blindsided!

So enjoy, be safe and come back in November for more. This is my favorite time of year (well, the beginning of it, anyway).

Regards,

Gail Chasan
Senior Editor

Please address questions and book requests to:
Silhouette Reader Service
U.S.: 3010 Walden Ave., P.O. Box 1325, Buffalo, NY 14269
Canadian: P.O. Box 609, Fort Erie, Ont. L2A 5X3

ADDING TO THE FAMILY

GINA WILKINS

Silhouette

SPECIAL EDITION

Published by Silhouette Books

America's Publisher of Contemporary Romance

As always, to my own loving and supportive family—
John, Courtney, Kerry and David.
Love you all.

 SILHOUETTE BOOKS

ISBN 0-373-24712-5

ADDING TO THE FAMILY

Copyright © 2005 by Gina Wilkins

Visit Silhouette Books at www.eHarlequin.com

Printed in U.S.A.

GINA WILKINS

It's Jared and Cassie Walker's twenty-fifth wedding anniversary and you are cordially invited to the biggest bash in Texas!

After decades of caring and support for their friends and family, we want to honor these two lovebirds.

So, come one, come all to celebrate on the Walker Ranch, Saturday, October 15th!

RSVP with Molly and Shane Walker

Prologue

Molly Walker appeared in the barn door with the early April afternoon sunlight behind her, making her long, red-streaked hair shine almost as brightly as her smile. "I have the most spectacular idea!"

Her half brother, Shane, and the horse he had been grooming looked around with almost identically wary expressions. "It always gives me a headache when you say that," Shane muttered.

Undaunted, Molly came all the way inside the barn to stand in front of him. "Trust me, this is a really good plan, and you barely have to do anything. I can take care of most of it myself."

The lanky cowboy dropped the curry brush on a

shelf and seemed to brace himself before asking, "Just what is it I barely have to do?"

Molly's dark green eyes held an expression of reproof when she shook a finger at him. "Stop overdramatizing. It isn't as if I've ever asked you to do anything *that* complicated."

Shane shared a comical look of disbelief with his beloved mare. *"Riiight."*

Molly slapped his arm playfully. "Anyway, you know Mom and Dad's twenty-fifth wedding anniversary is coming up in October."

"I remember their wedding. I was a teenager, after all. Just as I remember you being born a year and a couple of weeks later."

Shane and his father, Jared Walker, had been a couple of footloose bachelors before they'd encountered Cassie Browning and had both fallen head over heels in love with her. Nearly twenty-five years later, they were still a close and happy family, even though Shane had been married for almost ten years now and had two daughters of his own.

It was that loving family relationship that Molly wanted to commemorate in a big way. "We should plan a surprise anniversary party for them."

"Okay—that sounds normal enough. What's the catch?"

"No catch. They're planning that trip to Europe in early October, right? So while they're gone, we can get everything in place and we'll welcome them back with a big silver anniversary barbecue."

Shane looked almost relieved. "Yeah, we can do something like that. Kelly and I will help you plan it. I'm sure Aunt Layla and Aunt Michelle would be thrilled to help with the arrangements. Not to mention the assorted other aunts, uncles and cousins who jump at any chance to get together for a party."

Since Jared had five siblings, all married with offspring, any party the Walker clan put together was a big one. But Molly didn't intend to limit this bash merely to family. "We'll invite the D'Alessandros, of course."

Jared's sister, Michelle, had married private investigator Tony D'Alessandro not long before Jared and Cassie had married. Tony's large and boisterous family had been a part of Molly's life from the beginning. Her cousin Brynn, the daughter of Jared's deceased younger brother, Miles, had married another D'Alessandro, drawing the bond between the two families even tighter.

"And I want to invite the foster sons Mom and Dad took in during the earlier years—back before the ranch became a youth facility. Won't they love seeing them all together again for this special occasion?"

"We can definitely invite the ones we've kept in touch with. There's no way we can assume they'll all be here, of course."

"No, I want as many as possible here," she insisted. "Even the ones we haven't heard from in a while. I'm hoping to have at least a dozen of them."

"There are several we haven't heard from in years— Mark and Daniel and Kyle, for example. They were special to Dad and Cassie, but we don't even know where they are now."

"We'll find them." She flashed another confident smile. "We have uncles who own a private investigation agency, remember? With Uncle Tony, Uncle Joe, and Uncle Ryan helping us, I bet we'll have all the guys located within a few weeks."

"Maybe," Shane agreed, as confident as she was in their uncle's abilities, "but finding them doesn't guarantee they'll want to return here. Not everyone has fond memories of the past, you know, especially when that past includes a stint in foster care—as you could ask Dad or most of his siblings."

Molly tossed her head, making her mane of red-and-gold streaked hair swirl around her determined face. "Once the uncles find them, I'll talk them into being here."

"*If* anyone can, I suppose it would be you."

"Absolutely. Trust me, Shane, this is going to be the best anniversary party ever. Mom and Dad are going to be so surprised."

"I hope you aren't too disappointed if everything isn't perfect, Molly. You just might be in for a few surprises yourself, trying to plan something this big."

Waving a dismissive hand, Molly turned to head toward the main house on the sprawling Walker ranch not far from Dallas, Texas. She had lists to make, and a million things to do to pull off the perfect twenty-fifth anniversary party by October.

Chapter One

There was something about a man with a calculator that Miranda Martin found oddly sexy. A man whose fingers flew over a number pad, adding up columns of dollar amounts as he talked about bonds and investments and tax-deferred annuities—just the mental image could make her shiver with exhilaration.

Other women were attracted to cowboys or cops or bikers or baseball players; Miranda was a sucker for accountants. One accountant, in particular. Her own.

Her chin cupped in both hands, she rested her elbows on his desk and gazed across the glossy surface at him. It didn't hurt that he was so very nice to look at. Mark Wallace had clear gray eyes, disheveled brown hair with a tendency to curl into loose waves, and the most perfect teeth she'd ever seen. Had he not chosen to work with numbers, he could probably have made a living as a model.

"What's this deduction you're claiming for comfortable shoes?" he asked, frowning at the paperwork in front of him.

"I had to buy them on a business trip last month. The shoes I took with me were killing me, and you know you can't really concentrate on business when your feet hurt. I was much more effective after I bought those nice, comfy shoes—which, I might add, were obscenely expensive."

He had been her accountant for just over a year, and he always gave her exactly the same look when she said something he considered outrageous. He was giving her that look now, and she enjoyed it immensely. She had anticipated that expression when she had listed the deduction she had known very well his sharp eyes would not overlook.

He stared at her with his head cocked slightly to one side, as if he weren't quite sure if she was joking, and then he shook his head and marked through the item with a decisive stroke of his mechanical pencil.

She just loved it when he did that.

"Other than the shoes, everything looks to be in order," he remarked, closing the file folder. "I'll have the tax forms ready for your signature by the end of the week. Next time, though, you might not want to wait until the last minute to bring your information to me. You didn't allow either of us much room for error."

"As if you ever make any errors," she teased.

He shrugged, a smile playing at one corner of his firm mouth. "It's been known to happen—on very rare occasions."

Sometimes she couldn't resist touching him. She reached out to stroke a fingertip across the top of his right hand—the one that had just been calculating her money. "I find it hard to believe you aren't completely perfect."

Maybe after a year of working with her, he was finally getting accustomed to her flirting. He had been amusingly disconcerted the first couple of times, but during their meetings since, he'd seemed to accept it as part of the package. Especially since she had teasingly informed him that talking about money always gave her goose bumps.

In response to her stroking his hand, he shot her a look that was so direct, so male—and so uncharacteristically predatory—that her mouth suddenly went dry. "Someday I might just take you up on one of those come-hither looks," he murmured. "And then what are you going to do?"

For just a moment, Miranda Martin—who always had a witty put-down in response to even the most insistent advance—couldn't think of anything to say. She found herself lost in Mark Wallace's gleaming gray eyes, her mind filled with unsummoned and decidedly erotic images rather than cleverly cutting retorts.

Fine, take me up on it, she would have liked to say. *Heck, just take* me.

But she didn't say it, and the primary reason for her reticence burst into Mark's home-based office only a moment later.

"Daddy, I'm home from preschool and guess what? We're going on a field trip to the Museum of Discovery and I—"

"Payton," Mark cut in firmly, raising his voice a bit to be heard over the little blond girl's excited chattering. "I'm with a client. You know better than to come into my office when I'm working. Where's Mrs. McSwaim?"

Only slightly chastened, the blue-eyed, curly haired moppet pointed behind her while studying Miranda from the other side of the room. "She took Madison to the bathroom."

"Then go entertain yourself for a little while and I'll hear all about your field trip when I've finished with my work."

"Okay, Daddy." Heaving a dramatic sigh, Payton turned toward the doorway at the back of the office through which she had entered so precipitously.

Mark waited until the door closed behind his daughter, then swiveled his leather chair around to face Miranda again. "Sorry about that. Most of the time a home office has its advantages, but occasional interruptions come with the territory."

Miranda had her brightly impersonal smile firmly in place again. She reached down to the floor beside her chair, picked up her purse and slung it over her shoulder as she stood. "I've got to be going, anyway. I've got a few more work-related things to do before I make it to the concert at Juanita's tonight."

He nodded. "I'll call when the forms are ready."

She fluttered her lashes at him. "You do that."

"Have a good time at the concert."

"Darlin', I always have a good time." She made sure the smile that accompanied her huskily drawled reply held a touch of wickedness.

Just because there was no way she and Mark would ever have even a passing fling, it wouldn't hurt to leave him—like herself—wishing just a little that things could be different between them.

Of all Mark's clients, there was only one who left his head spinning after every meeting, no matter how briskly professional he tried to keep things between them.

Miranda Martin.

He thought of her as "the golden girl." Her almost shoulder-length, layered chestnut hair was shot through with artfully applied golden highlights. Her flawless skin was deepened either by tanning booths or bronzers. Even her eyes were a pure amber—and those he suspected were her natural color.

She had a smooth forehead, a perfect nose, high cheekbones and a rounded chin dotted with a shallow dimple just below the right corner of her mouth. Of medium height, she had legs that went on forever, nicely proportioned breasts, a slim waist and gently curving hips—adding up to a package that would make any red-blooded man stop in his tracks and think, *Whoa, buddy!*

If he were a man who was interested in fleeting affairs, he would have taken her up on the invitation her habitual flirting seemed to imply long ago. But he was the full-time single father of two little girls. He didn't have the time nor the luxury to indulge in affairs.

As for anything else—well, he'd been married to a woman who had valued entertainment above the daily responsibilities of family life. Even if he were in the market for a long-term relationship, it wouldn't be with a party girl like Miranda Martin.

Besides, he had seen the way she'd looked at his kids on the rare occasion when she'd seen them. As if strange and somewhat intimidating aliens had wandered into her field of vision. Even if he tried to delude himself into thinking he and Miranda could form a personal bond, he had a feeling that she considered there to be two very prominent obstacles in their path.

"Who was that lady in your office today, Daddy?" Payton asked over dinner that evening.

"You mean the one you so rudely interrupted when you burst in without knocking?"

She sighed—something she did with innately expressive skill. "I already said I'm sorry," she reminded him. "Who was she?"

"A client. Her name is Miranda Martin."

"She was pretty."

Mark glanced across the table. "Madison, don't give your peas to Poochie. Eat them yourself."

Three-year-old Madison, a smaller, blonder duplicate of her sister, obligingly stuffed a spoonful of peas into her food-smeared mouth, leaving Poochie, a rather ragged stray mutt Mark had rescued six months earlier, to wait beneath the table in hopes of dropped scraps.

Payton, who liked to tell everyone she was four-going-on-five (in just four months), and whom Mark thought of as four-going-on-thirty, wasn't finished asking questions. "Don't you think she's pretty, Daddy?"

Mark was still keeping a watchful eye on his youngest child. "Mmm? You mean Madison? I think she's very pretty."

Payton groaned. "Not Madison, Daddy. That lady. Miranda Martin."

That reclaimed his attention. "Yeah, sure. She's very pretty."

"Can I get my ears pierced? I want some of those big gold circles like she had."

Picturing his four-year-old in gypsy hoops, Mark stifled a smile. "Not until you're older."

"Nicola Cooper got pierced ears. She gets to wear little silver circles."

"When you're older, Payton."

Another sigh, and then, "Are you going to take her on a date?"

"No."

"Nicola Cooper's mother goes on dates. She gets all dressed up in pretty clothes and takes Nicola to her grandma's house. Sometimes Nicola gets to stay all night at her grandma's house."

"Yes, well…eat your chicken, babe. It's getting cold."

Two hastily swallowed bites later, Payton was at it again. "Why aren't you going to take her on a date if you think she's pretty?"

"Just because." As an answer, it was pretty lame, but the best he could come up with at the moment. "Tell me more about your field trip," he said, making an attempt to change the subject. "When did you say you're going? Next Monday?"

He remembered perfectly well that it was Tuesday, but at least the question distracted Payton from his social life—or lack thereof. She started chattering about the planned outing, seeming to forget all about Miranda Martin.

Mark wished *he* could forget her as quickly. Payton's innocent questions had made him think of things that would be much better left alone.

Though Little Rock was the capitol and the largest city in Arkansas, it was still small enough that Miranda could hardly go anywhere without running into someone she knew. Especially at the local music clubs where she liked to hang out in the evenings; she only had to walk in for someone to call out to her to join them at their table.

Tonight that table included three other women and two men, all of whom Miranda knew at least in passing. She considered them friends, though she doubted that any one of them would be of much use if she found herself in trouble. Not that it mattered to her, since she considered herself a fiercely independent woman who took care of her own problems and expected others to do the same.

"Miranda, you look amazing," Oliver Cartwright pronounced, studying her outfit with a critical eye. "Not many people can get away with that color, but it looks fabulous on you."

"Coming from you, that's a high compliment," she assured him.

She had paid a little extra attention to her appearance tonight, pairing a flirty gold top with a pair of low-slung dark jeans and strappy heels. The top was cut just low enough at the neckline to give a glimpse of cleavage and just high enough at the hem to reveal an inch of spray-tanned abdomen. Modest compared to what many of the young women in the club were wearing, but still eye-catching, which had been her intention.

If Oliver, the local fashion cop, approved, she must have done something right, she thought with satisfaction.

"Lucky you," a busty bottle-blonde in a clingy red dress said with a pout. "Oliver said *I* look like an over-ripe tomato."

"You insist on wearing clothes that are too tight for you," he pointed out to her. "I keep telling you that subtlety is sexier than a desperate play for attention."

"Miranda's wearing a shiny gold top. Isn't that a play for attention?"

"Note that Miranda's boobs aren't trying their best to escape the fabric that covers them. You'll certainly get attention with your dress tonight, Brandi, but don't come crying to us again when the Mr. Right Now you take home disappears with the sunrise."

Brandi, who made no secret of her desire to get married—preferably to someone with money—flounced discontentedly in her seat. "You're so mean, Oliver."

"Yes, darling, but I'm always right."

The rest of the party laughed at his droll retort, though no one dared dispute it.

A cocktail waitress appeared at the table and Miranda ordered a Manhattan while several of the others requested seconds of their own drinks. She would allow herself only a single drink tonight, but she would thoroughly savor that one indulgence.

Having grown up in a home where alcohol was synonymous with sin—as were dancing, cursing, television, movies, fiction, vanity, frivolity and any sexual activity, including handholding and kissing, outside of marriage—she had vowed to be answerable to no one but herself when she escaped, which she had done after graduating from high school at seventeen. That was ten years ago, and she hadn't looked back since.

Oliver turned back to his friend Randall, and Brandi strutted off to the ladies' room, making sure she caught plenty of male attention on the way. An attractive woman Miranda had met a couple of times before leaned over to ask quietly, "Do you think he hurt her feelings?"

"Brandi? Hardly. She'll sulk awhile, then she'll go home with some guy who'll treat her exactly as Oliver predicted, and next week she'll start the whole cycle again. She always insists on asking Oliver what he thinks of her clothes, even though she has to know what he's going to say."

Someone else interrupted that conversation. "Hey, Miranda, what do you know about entertaining kids?"

She turned to the brunette on her left. "As little as possible. Why do you ask, Bev?"

Bev shrugged. "My brother's bringing his three kids to visit Mom next month, when school's out, and she's asked me to help entertain them. You always know something fun to do. I thought you might have some ideas."

"Honey, my ideas never involve children," Miranda returned with an exaggerated shudder.

A round of laughter answered her words.

"What?" someone asked. "No nieces or nephews?"

She started to shake her head, and then she stopped herself. "Oh, wait. I do have a couple of nephews."

Oliver raised his carefully arched blond eyebrows. "You forgot you're an aunt?"

"I don't think of myself as an aunt," she said with a slight shrug. "I haven't seen the kids more than a couple of times in their lives—my sister doesn't stay in one place for very long."

"My brother's the same way," someone else said. "I wouldn't mind seeing my nieces, actually, but they're living in Singapore now, if you can believe it. My brother has a fabulous job there. He—"

Not particularly interested, Miranda tuned out and took a sip of her drink, thinking about her older sister for the first time in ages. She wondered where Lisa was these days, and whether she was taking any better care of her five-year-old twins than she had been the last time she'd breezed through town, hoping to bum a few dollars from Miranda.

The idea of having her own children made Miranda practically choke with claustrophobic panic. Nothing would be more certain to put an end to the carefree, independent lifestyle she had spent her entire youth plotting to achieve.

Maybe Lisa didn't mind dragging her conceived-by-accident twins around on her own reckless adventures, but Miranda had always firmly believed that if someone was going to bring children into the world, the kids' well-being should come first—unlike her own parents, of course. Being childless, she could be as self-centered and irresponsible as she liked, and no one would have to suffer for it.

She couldn't help thinking for a moment about her sexy accountant. Mark Wallace seemed like a good father, stable and loving and dependable. She didn't know what had happened to his kids' mother, but Mark seemed to have committed himself completely to making sure his girls had a happy childhood and a decent upbringing, even if it meant his own life was a bit dull, in Miranda's opinion. Still, she had to admire his dedication.

Unfortunately for the twins' sakes, Lisa had a different view of parenting than Mark, or even Miranda. Lisa saw no reason for motherhood to interfere with her lifestyle in the least.

There had been no fun in their own childhoods, Lisa had reminded Miranda the last time they had seen each other. Her kids were going to have fun. No horribly restrictive rules, no rigid schedules, no harsh punishments if they didn't toe some arbitrary and impossible line.

The boys were probably monsters, but that was Lisa's problem, Miranda thought with a shrug. Miranda had an evening of music and camaraderie to enjoy, and she was wasting time thinking about serious matters.

Chapter Two

By Thursday of that week, Miranda was uncharacter-istically restless. There wasn't much going on at the moment in her job as an assistant buyer for Little Rock-based Ballard's Department Stores. She had been to a club nearly every night for the past two weeks, and she wasn't in the mood that night. But she didn't want to sit in her tiny apartment and watch TV, either.

She checked the messages on her machine when she arrived home from work, hoping maybe someone would have an idea for an evening's entertainment that intrigued her. Brandi's was the first voice she heard. "Hi, Miranda, it's me. There's going to be a new band at Vino's tonight and I heard the lead singer is really hot. Some of us will be there around eight if you want to join us."

"I don't think so." Miranda erased that message and moved on to the next.

"Yo, 'Randa, it's Robbie. I haven't heard from you in a couple of weeks. What, did you drop off the face of the earth or somepin?" He chuckled at his own wit, then continued, "Anyway, babe, I'd love to see you again, so why don't you give me a call and we'll go party, yo? You've got my cell number."

"No, actually, I tossed it." Miranda punched the erase button again. She had gone out with Robbie once, but she had no interest in seeing him again. Last time he'd been so grabby she'd finished the evening with unwelcome fingerprints all over her body. She didn't care for the steamroller approach to seduction, and she had made it quite clear to Robbie that *she* would be the one to decide when—or if—their casual dating took the next step.

She had decided it wouldn't. Robbie was history.

The next male voice that issued from her answering machine was as brusquely businesslike as Robbie's had been presumptuously intimate, but this time Miranda's knees showed a distinct inclination to jellify. "Hi, Miranda, it's Mark Wallace. I have your tax returns ready. You can stop by my office anytime tomorrow to sign them. If I'm tied up, my assistant can take care of everything for you."

Lordy, but Mark Wallace had a voice that could make a woman's heart get an aerobic workout, Miranda mused, her finger hovering over the erase button. Warm, deep, with just a faintly rough edge, his was a voice that made her fantasize about sweet nothings and pillow talk. Okay, so the man was off-limits—but there was nothing wrong with a little fantasizing, right?

She indulged herself for a few minutes in a pleasantly naughty daydream involving his big, glossy desk. And then she sighed regretfully and made herself push the erase button.

She finally decided to take in a movie—alone. There were times when she just didn't feel particularly social, and this was one of them. She would be surrounded by people, but she wouldn't have to make conversation with any of them. Perfect for her mood tonight.

There were only a few theater choices in Little Rock. She drove to the one she usually patronized, since it provided stadium-style seating and what she considered the best popcorn in town.

She wanted a film that was mindless, noisy and action-filled, with a high pretty-boy factor. There was just such a movie playing this evening. She stood in a line filled mostly with teenagers and bought her ticket, then joined another line to buy popcorn and a drink.

Clutching her snacks, she turned away from the counter and almost ran smack dab into Mark Wallace. Talk about coincidences…

Holding a blond toddler on his left hip and the hand of his older daughter in his right hand, Mark looked as surprised as Miranda was to see him.

"This is really freaky," she said. "I just heard your voice on my machine less than an hour ago."

He smiled. "It's certainly a coincidence. How are you?"

"Fine, thanks." Feeling herself being studied by two pairs of curious blue eyes, Miranda looked warily at the girls. She should probably say something to them, but she wasn't sure what. She settled for a smile and a "hi."

"Miss Martin, these are my daughters, Payton and Madison."

Miranda smiled at the toddler who gazed so intently back at her, one forefinger stuck in her mouth. "Hello, Madison."

Madison buried her face in her father's neck.

Not as shy as her younger sister, Payton piped up, "You were in Daddy's office."

"Yes, I was. You came in to tell him about a field trip."

"I got in trouble for not knocking," Payton said, not looking particularly perturbed by the memory. Apparently the punishment hadn't been overly severe. "I like your earrings."

"Um, thanks." She was wearing a pair of her favored gold hoops. "I like your shirt," she said, nodding toward the sparkly butterfly on the girl's pink T-shirt.

"It's new. Would you tell my daddy to let me get pierced ears like you and Nicola Cooper?"

Miranda didn't have a clue who Nicola Cooper was, but she knew better than to interfere in a parental decision. "You're on your own with that battle, kiddo."

"Your hair has stripes in it," Payton announced, her eyes narrowing thoughtfully.

"They're called highlights, and before you ask, I can't help you there with your father, either."

"I don't think I want stripes. Just earrings."

Miranda laughed at the kid's candor. "I really should introduce you to my friend Oliver sometime. I think the two of you would get along very well."

Mark abruptly cleared his throat. "We'd better be going. It's Madison's bedtime."

"You've already seen a movie?"

"Yeah. We do the early showings. The kids brought me to see the new animated film that came out today."

"It's his birthday," Payton confided. "Daddy's thirty. We had cake."

So Mark had spent his thirtieth birthday watching a cartoon movie with two kids under five. She wondered wryly how he could stand the excitement. "Happy birthday, Mark."

"Thanks. But don't let us keep you any longer. I'm sure your companion is waiting for you."

"No companion tonight. I came stag."

He lifted an eyebrow as he glanced at the big tub of popcorn and large diet soda in her arms.

"All mine," she informed him loftily. "When I splurge, I go all out."

"So I see. Well…enjoy."

"Thanks."

"Bye, Miss Martin," Payton called over her shoulder as her father led her away.

"Goodbye, Payton. And Madison," she added, earning a quick, shy smile from the smaller girl before she promptly ducked into her daddy's shoulder again.

Very strange encounter, Miranda mused as she settled into a theater seat and placed her soda in the cup holder. It was pretty startling to see Mark in his role as doting dad right after he'd played the part of hunky accountant in her erotic daydream.

One would think she would find him less appealing in that light, considering the way she felt about kids. Funny thing was, she had been just as strangely drawn to him as ever.

When it came to Mark Wallace, Miranda couldn't even predict her own reactions. There was nothing wrong with a little fantasy, she reminded herself. She just had to remember not to get those harmless daydreams mixed up with reality.

Mark had half hoped that Miranda would pick up her tax forms while he was occupied with another client. It wasn't that he didn't appreciate the sight of her. Seeing her was always like having a few extra rays of sunshine brighten his day.

Yet it was that very type of imagery that made him increasingly wary of seeing her too often. His life wasn't what anyone would call exciting, but he had been content with it for the past couple of years. He didn't need anyone messing with his mind, making him wish for something more than what he had now.

A caregiver. That was what he had always been, and what he would likely always be. From the time he was just a kid, taking care of his chronically ill mother and his little sister, he had been compelled to help people who needed him. Too many times he had reached out a hand and pulled back a bloody stump—at least that was what it had felt like to him when people he'd tried to help had turned on him with a vengeance. His ex-wife, for example.

Now his daughters needed him. He was all they had and taking care of them required all his concentration. All his energy. He did his best to help his clients with their financial needs, but he didn't get overly involved with any of them. The only one who even tempted him to do so was Miranda.

So, he wasn't sure whether he was pleased or per-turbed when she arrived at his office just after his last appointment for the day had departed.

Two years earlier, Mark had set up for business in his west Little Rock home, converting a side door into the office entrance. That door led into a small reception area that held a love seat, two visitor chairs and his assistant's desk and credenza. Mark's smallish, but adequate-size workspace opened off that room, with another door behind him that led into the house.

The setup worked well for him, keeping him close to his kids even during the busiest times of the year. He often returned to the office after the girls were asleep, leaving the door to the house open so he could hear them if they needed him. He would never get rich with his one-man CPA business, but he was supporting his family, and that was all that mattered to him.

"Ms. Martin is here for her returns," his assistant announced from the open doorway very late that afternoon. "She said she would like to speak with you, if you have a few minutes."

He resisted an impulse to smooth his hair, which was typically tousled at this time of day, thanks to his habit of running a hand through it when he concentrated on something. "Sure, Pam. Send her in."

"Okay. And unless you need me for anything, I'm gone for the day."

"No, go ahead. I'll see you Monday. Have a nice weekend."

"Thanks. You, too."

A moment later Miranda appeared in the doorway where Pam had stood. She wore a bright pink top with black slacks. For someone who had claimed to hate it when her feet hurt, she sure seemed to have a thing for trendy shoes, he thought, glancing at the heeled, narrow boots she was wearing.

Only then did he notice that she was carrying a cheerfully wrapped present in her left hand. She came in singing the happy birthday song and set the package on his desk in front of him.

A little flustered, he rose. "This wasn't necessary."

She dropped into a chair. "Just open it."

Sitting behind the desk again, he tore away the wrapping paper from her gift to reveal a bottle of liquor. One glance at the label made him do a double-take. "Whoa."

"As much as you probably enjoyed the outing with

your kids, I figured you needed something grown-up to commemorate your thirtieth birthday."

"This is too much," he said with a dazed shake of his head. "You shouldn't have—"

"Hey, Wallace. Just because you count my money doesn't mean you can tell me how to spend it. Just say, thank you, Miranda."

He sighed. "Thank you, Miranda."

"Good boy." She grinned at him, and it was impossible to resist smiling back.

"How was your movie?" he asked to change the subject.

She shrugged. "Loud. Predictable. I enjoyed it—but mostly I enjoyed the popcorn."

He reached into a wire basket on his credenza and plucked out a file. "Sign where I've stuck the flags and I'll file the forms electronically. You should receive your federal and state refunds within the next few weeks."

"Oh, yeah, I can party then," she murmured sarcastically as she flipped to the flagged pages and signed her name.

Shaking his head, he replied, "As I've told you several times, it's better to pay less up-front and keep your money in the bank than overpay and get a bigger refund at the end of the year. The government doesn't pay interest. And aren't you even going to look those over? You can take them home, you know, though I have to have them back by closing time tomorrow."

"I trust you," she said, closing the file that held her

copies without another glance at them. "I wouldn't pay you to do this for me if I didn't."

"I wouldn't trust *anyone* that much with my tax forms," he said in a chiding tone. "I'd have to check to make sure everything was done the way I wanted it to be."

She didn't seem at all shaken in her confidence. "Got a bit of OCD, do we?"

"Obsessive compulsive disorder? Maybe a little. Must be why I chose to be an accountant—just to make sure all the columns add up and the bottom lines balance."

He was unreasonably pleased when she laughed.

She stood to hand the signed forms back to him, leaning slightly across the desk as she offered it. Her bright pink top gapped a bit with the movement, and he was treated to a clear view of the tops of her creamy breasts. He didn't believe it was intentional on her part, but the fact that he was still seated put him directly at eye level with her chest. And a nice chest it was, he noted before he quickly glanced away.

He shifted uncomfortably in his chair. It had been too long since he had spent an adult night out if he was reacting this strongly to a glimpse of cleavage.

"I suppose you have big plans for the weekend?" he asked as Miranda took her seat again, apparently in no hurry to leave.

"No, not really. I'm just going to play it by ear."

"Maybe I could buy you dinner tomorrow night?" It had been a while since he had asked anyone out, and his awkwardness now made that painfully clear. It wasn't as if he had given any thought to the invitation, since he'd blurted it out almost before he had realized he was going to ask.

For the first time since he had met her, he saw Miranda Martin at a temporary loss for words. "Is this like a thank-you-for-your-business dinner?" she asked after a moment.

"Not exactly. But I'll understand if you don't want to mix business with pleasure." It was a risk he probably shouldn't be taking himself, actually. Maybe it would be better all around if she turned him down. He'd have gotten the urge to ask out of his system, and she would have made it clear she wasn't interested, putting a stop to any further imaginings on his part.

Miranda toyed with the folder in her lap, studying him with atypically somber eyes. "It isn't that I'm not tempted. I think dinner with you could be fun. But you should know that I make it a rule not to get involved with a man with kids."

"And I'm not looking to get involved with anyone, either," he returned. "Precisely because of those kids. That doesn't mean I don't appreciate an occasional adult evening out."

"So you're just suggesting a casual date?"

"Just dinner," he agreed. "I spent my birthday watching a cartoon with two preschoolers. It would be nice to have a conversation that doesn't center around animated characters or talking animals."

As he watched her mentally debate the invitation for

a few moments longer, he wondered what was going through her mind.

"Okay, sure," she said finally. "We'll call it a birthday dinner. But in that case, I should pay."

He tapped the bottle of expensive liquor sitting on his desk. "I'd say you've spent enough already. Dinner will be my treat. Dress comfortably—I have no intention of wearing a tie. I'm celebrating my birthday and the end of tax season."

She smiled. "Fine. You can write the expense off, anyway. Remind me to ask you an accounting question sometime during the meal."

He chuckled and escorted her out of his office, agreeing to the details of the dinner date along the way. And then he returned to his desk, where he wasted the next half hour wondering what on earth he'd been thinking when he had impulsively asked out Miranda Martin.

Miranda was almost ready the next evening when her telephone rang. Her first thought was that Mark had changed his mind—come to his senses, maybe. Her second thought was, damn, she'd spent the past hour primping for nothing.

"Hello?"

"Hi. It's me."

"Lisa?" This was more of a surprise than having Mark cancel dinner. Miranda could hardly remember the last time she had spoken with her sister. "Are you here in town?"

"No. But, Miranda, I'm in trouble."

Miranda resisted an urge to groan. "How much do you need?"

"No, it's worse than that."

Something in her sister's voice made a chill run down Miranda's spine. "Lisa, what's wrong? What do you need me to do?"

"I just—I just want you to know I'm sorry. And I wish things had been different—for both of us. I really do love you, you know. I've always been able to turn to you when I needed you. And since Grandma died, you're the only one in our family I can say that about."

Miranda was getting more anxious by the moment. "Please, tell me what's going on. Are you ill? Is something wrong with the boys?"

"I'm so sorry, Miranda. I need you again. It's the biggest favor I've ever asked of you, but I know you'll do the right thing."

"I don't know what you're talking about. Tell me—"

"Damn, I've got to go." There was a new note of tension in Lisa's voice now, which had dropped to little more than a whisper. "Please, Miranda, don't let me down."

"Wait, you haven't even told me what—"

But Lisa had already hung up, and when Miranda tried the call return function, the phone number was blocked.

She slammed down the telephone receiver in frustration. Lisa had always been prone to melodrama, but this mysterious call was unusual even for her. Miranda just hoped her older sister hadn't done anything really stupid this time, though considering the tone of that telephone call, it seemed to be a futile wish.

Now she was running late and Mark was due any minute. Growling beneath her breath, she dashed for her bedroom—not exactly a long run since her two-room apartment was somewhat smaller than tiny.

She had just slipped her feet into her shoes when her doorbell rang. Fluffing her hair with one hand, she made a quick mirror-check before heading for the door.

She had debated what to wear, wanting to dress up a bit more than her usual weekend jeans, but not wanting to look as though she had put too much effort into her grooming. She had settled on a three-quarter sleeve sunshine-yellow blouse worn open over a white tank top and a short denim skirt with a wide leather belt at the hips. Leather wedge-heeled sandals and chunky gold and amber jewelry completed the casual outfit. Now she was rethinking her choices. Maybe she should have worn—

Bringing an abrupt stop to that line of thought, she shook her head at her uncharacteristic hesitation and opened the door.

Mark looked as delectable as always in a hunter-green cotton shirt and khakis. Admittedly more conservative than her usual crowd, but sexy enough to make her pulse rate increase, anyway.

"You look very nice," he said, giving her a smile that held just a touch of shy awkwardness. Which, of course, only endeared him more to her.

"Thank you."

He glanced around her miniscule, thrift-store furnished apartment. "Nice place. It's very...cozy."

"Which is your tactful way of pointing out how small it is." She shrugged. "I would rather spend my extra money on fun than rent."

Because he knew exactly how much she made, and how much she stashed into savings for a future in which she intended to retire young and spend a great deal of time traveling, he didn't seem surprised by that choice. "It's still a nice place."

"Thanks." She slung her purse over her shoulder and locked the door behind them as they headed outside.

This evening could be very interesting. Either she would find out that Mark Wallace wasn't the stimulating company she had imagined he would be, or the night would end with her being just as fascinated by him as she had been to this point.

She figured she could handle whatever happened between them as long as neither one of them showed signs of getting too serious.

Chapter Three

Mark couldn't remember being so nervous about a date since high school. It annoyed him that he was acting more like a teenager than a thirty-year-old father of two.

Maybe the problem was that he hadn't dated much since his divorce just over two years ago. He had been too busy setting up his home-based accounting practice and raising two little girls, who had been barely more than babies when his ex-wife had left.

On the handful of occasions he had gone out during the past couple of years—usually at the urging of a friend who had someone he just *had* to meet—the women he had seen had been very different from

Miranda. More subdued. More conservative. Usually divorced, themselves, and busy raising children of their own.

Mark hadn't really clicked with any of them. As nice as they had been, he was usually relieved when the awkward evenings had ended and he'd been back at home. Was he really such a glutton for punishment that he was attracted only to women who were completely wrong for him?

"You're kind of quiet tonight," Miranda commented after their food was placed in front of them.

Worried that he hadn't been holding up his end of the conversation, he forced a smile. "Sorry. This time of year, most accountants go into brain overload."

"I can imagine. Especially if all your clients are as late getting their paperwork to you as I was."

"Not everyone waits so late—but enough to make this season a challenge."

"I bet."

Mark sliced into his steak. "You're a bit quieter than usual, yourself."

"Sorry. Just before you arrived this evening, I had a disturbing phone call."

He frowned. "Not bad news, I hope."

She toyed with her lemon-peppered salmon, her expression solemn. "No. Or maybe. I'm not really sure, actually."

Bemused, he tilted his head to study her face. "You're not sure?"

"With my sister, it's hard to tell sometimes."

He grimaced. "Now that's a remark I understand completely."

"You have a sister?"

"Yep."

"Older or younger?"

"Younger. And if she lives to be my age, it will be a miracle."

"And that's a remark *I* understand completely."

"Your sister's a risk-taker, too?"

Miranda rolled her eyes. "Risk-taker is a bit tame when it comes to describing Lisa. Lisa takes unpredictability to extremes. She's rarely in the same place two months in a row, she's never with the same guy for more than a few weeks, she's always just one step away from total financial disaster. If I didn't...well—"

"You slip her some money occasionally?" he guessed when she stopped.

Miranda shrugged. "I do, and so do other people. She seems to attract people who like to give her things, especially men. But they never seem to stay around long. She has trouble keeping jobs. And hanging on to money. I can't let her go hungry, not to mention her kids."

"Kids?" At least *his* sister wasn't dragging children around on her adventures. "How many does she have?"

"Two. Twin boys."

"Yeah? How old?"

"Five. I think," she added with a frown of uncertainty.

He felt his eyebrows rise. "You don't know how old your nephews are?"

"I'm pretty sure they were five in February. They were born on Valentine's Day—I remember that because Lisa made such a big deal out of it. And why does everyone act like I should know everything about my sister's kids? I've only seen them a couple of times in their whole lives."

Because she was starting to sound defensive, he held up a hand. "I didn't mean anything by it. How could you know them if you never see them?"

"Exactly. Does your sister have kids?"

"No. Terry has never married. She's a photojournalist who travels all over the world—generally to the most dangerous spots she can find."

"Lisa never married, either. The boys came from an affair she had with someone she barely remembers."

"Does he know about his sons?"

"She told him. He wasn't interested. He gave her a sizable check, then disappeared from her life. She went through the money before the twins were out of diapers."

"It must have been tough for her, having two infants to care for. Did your parents help her?"

Miranda almost snorted. "Hardly. Our parents are the two most rigid, judgmental, dictatorial people on earth. They disowned Lisa when she left home the day after her high school graduation to get away from them. They did the same to me when I left home two years later. I was almost eighteen. Unlike Lisa, I had a college scholarship—full tuition and room and board paid. I was lucky. Between that and several part-time retail jobs, I was able to earn my degree in four and a half years. I've been working for Ballard's ever since."

"Sounds like you and your sister are opposites in many ways. She drifts, you've stayed in the same job. She spends money and you save. She lives for the present, while you plan for the future. She has her twins and you stay far away from kids."

"That pretty well sums us up," she agreed with a slight shrug. "But we have several things in common, too. Neither of us will ever let ourselves be browbeaten or controlled by anyone again. And there's still a bond between us that was formed during those years when the only emotional support either of us had came from each other."

"Your parents are still living?"

"Yes. They're only in their early sixties."

"But you never see them?"

"No." She abruptly changed the subject to his family. "What about you? Are your parents still around?"

"My father died when I was just a kid. My mother was in poor health for many years. She died while I was in my last year of college, when Terry was a junior in high school. I watched out for Terry until she left for college. She's been on her own ever since, though she has always known I was here for her if she needed me."

"It sounds as though she was lucky to have you."

"We were lucky to have each other."

"You didn't mind taking care of your younger sister when you were fresh out of college?"

"No. I was all she had," he answered simply.

"Mr. Dependable," she murmured, then speared a tiny herbed carrot and lifted it to her smiling mouth.

He didn't appreciate the slight mockery he thought he detected in her tone. "The foster workers who labeled me a troublemaker would find it amusing to hear you call me that."

She swallowed too fast, then reached for her water glass. "You?" she asked a moment later. "A troublemaker? My buttoned-down, conservative, single-dad accountant?"

He wasn't sure why he was revealing so much of his past to her. Maybe it was because he hadn't engaged in much adult conversation lately, and he'd forgotten how to make small talk. Or because Miranda had looked so troubled when she had spoken of the call from her sister that he'd felt she needed a distraction. Or maybe he simply wanted her to see him as something more than her "buttoned-down, conservative, single-dad accountant."

"My mom got very sick the year I was fourteen and Terry was nine. Mom spent thirteen months in a hospital while Terry and I were sent to separate foster homes. We lived in Texas then, just outside of Dallas."

"And you didn't like the foster home where you were sent?"

"Hated it. I was determined to get back to my mom and sister. I thought they needed me to take care of them, you see. I ran away twice from that home, and then I was sent to another one, but I ran away from there, too. That's when I was labeled a troubled youth and sent to a ranch that specialized in taking in at-risk boys, no more than one or two at a time. I was the only one there during my stay."

At least they were keeping a conversation going now. Miranda seemed genuinely intrigued. "How did things work out for you at the ranch?"

"Very well, actually." He picked up his water glass as he thought back to a time he hadn't consciously remembered in years. "The couple who owned the ranch—Jared and Cassie Walker—were really good people. They had a son who was in college and a cute little red-haired daughter just a year younger than Terry. Jared was a no-nonsense cowboy who had a knack for asserting his authority without ever raising his voice. I pretty much idolized him by the end of my stay there."

Miranda propped her elbow on the table and rested her chin on her fist. "So you lived on a ranch for a year. Did you ride horses and rope cows and stuff?"

"Mostly 'stuff,'" he replied wryly. "I mucked out the stalls a lot."

"Eww."

"My sentiments, exactly. You'll notice I didn't pursue a ranching career, though I enjoyed my time there for the most part."

"Do you ever see your foster family now?"

"I haven't seen them since I was returned to my mother and sister when I was fifteen." He still clearly remembered that tearful reunion. His mother had been overjoyed to have her children with her again. She had been so devastated to be separated from them that she had burst into tears every time Mark had mentioned the ranch from that day on.

He had felt vaguely guilty that he had bonded with the Walker family during his stay there. That guilt had compelled him to put his memories of the ranch away. He hadn't responded to the Christmas or birthday cards Cassie had sent him, and eventually they had stopped coming. He had no idea if Jared and Cassie still lived on the ranch or if they remembered him. But the memories he had tucked away so deeply still warmed him on the rare occasions when he pulled them out.

"You're an interesting man, Mark Wallace," Miranda said, setting down her fork and pushing her plate away. "Darned good-looking, too. It's rather a shame that we won't be having a teeth-rattling affair. It might have been a memorable experience."

He refused to let her see that she had disconcerted him with her intentionally outrageous comment. Instead he looked her right in the eyes and spoke confidently, "Trust me, it would most definitely be a memorable experience. And you would get more than your teeth rattled."

He saw speculation enter her eyes, as if she were contemplating the same sort of images filling his mind at that moment. And then she smiled crookedly and shook her head, dropping her hand to her lap. "Maybe they were right to label you a troublemaker, after all. But as it happens, I'm not looking for trouble in my life just now."

"Nor am I," he said with a touch of regret. "So how about if we indulge in dessert, instead?"

She smiled at him from across the table. "Let's make that a truly sinful dessert. Since it's the only sin we'll be committing tonight."

Mark wasn't so sure about that. Not if she counted the dreams he would undoubtedly have about her as sinful, which he had no doubt they would be.

Mark drove Miranda straight home after they finished dinner. He said nothing about seeing her again during the brief drive, and she assumed he considered this outing a one-time event.

She wasn't sure what had prompted his invitation. Simple curiosity, perhaps. An impulsive gesture by a man who had been working too hard and spending too much time with preschoolers. She had found the evening both entertaining and illuminating. Who would have thought her accountant was a former bad boy?

Still, it was probably for the best if they kept their future encounters strictly business. Maybe Mark had been a rebel once, but he was Mr. Responsibility now. The most important women in his life were named Payton and Madison, and Miranda had no intention of competing with them for his attention.

No kids, she reminded herself. She had very good reasons for making that her number one rule when it came to dating.

He parked his family-sized SUV in an empty space at her apartment complex and turned off the engine. "I'll walk you to your door."

"I had a nice time tonight," she told him as they ambled toward her ground-floor apartment. "Thank you for the dinner."

"Was it really necessary for you to ask the restaurant staff to sing happy birthday to me when they delivered our desserts?"

She laughed at the embarrassment still lingering in his voice. "You must admit they were very enthusiastic about it. Their voices carried quite well, didn't they?"

Mark groaned. "Much too well, actually. I was ready to sink beneath the table."

She couldn't resist reaching out to take his arm in a companionable manner. "You were so cute. Your face was as red as the cherries on your cheesecake."

The wry look he slanted at her made her giggle, especially since his cheeks had turned a bit dark again. "I'm so glad you were entertained."

So maybe this was their one and only date. Maybe they were a mismatched couple. Still, the night wasn't quite over yet—and if it was their only outing together, they should definitely take a few memories away with them.

She paused in front of her door and turned to smile invitingly up at him. "There's one more birthday tradition I haven't taken care of yet."

"Yeah?" He looked suddenly wary. "You don't have a crowd of people waiting in the bushes to jump out and yell 'surprise,' do you?"

She laughed again and slid her hands up the front of his buttoned-down green shirt. "Actually I was thinking of the traditional birthday kiss."

"Were you, now?"

Oh, yeah, he was interested. She could see it in his narrowed gray eyes.

"Mmm. Just a little taste—" she walked her fingers up his chest "—to see what it might be like—" she moved a step closer to him "—if things had been different for us."

His mouth lowered slowly toward hers. "And what if that taste leaves me hungry for more?"

Their lips were almost close enough to meet when she murmured, "I've heard that self-denial builds character. But what harm can come from just a little taste?"

Their lips touched.

"Miss Martin? Miranda Martin?"

Both Mark and Miranda froze. And then Mark stepped back as Miranda turned to face the man who stood behind them on the sidewalk. The parking lot lights illuminated the hesitant expression on his broad, plain face.

"Yes, I'm Miranda Martin. Who are you?"

"My name is Jack Parsons. I'm an acquaintance of your sister's."

"Lisa?" Remembering the disturbing telephone call, Miranda felt her heart jump. "What's wrong? Has something happened to her?"

"No, she's okay. She wanted me to give you this." The man held out an envelope, his big hand not quite steady. "And I have a delivery for you in my car."

"A delivery?" Totally confused now, Miranda tilted her head to study him, trying without success to read the expression on the man's face.

"Yeah. I'll go get…I'll be right back," he stammered, moving backward.

Miranda turned to Mark. "This is weird, even for Lisa. I have no clue what's going on."

"I'll hang around until you find out," he said, frowning after the man who had interrupted them. "I'm not sure I trust that guy."

Miranda wasn't about to argue with him. She wasn't sure she trusted the man, either, even if he did claim to be a friend of Lisa's—or maybe because of that fact.

She was looking down at the envelope in her hand, tugging at the glued-down flap, when she heard Mark say in a rather odd voice, "Um, Miranda? Take a look at what the delivery is."

She looked up at him, frowned at the strange expression on his face, and then turned to see what he was staring at so intently. Her own jaw dropped. "Oh, no."

Jack Parsons was on his way back to her, dragging two large, wheeled suitcases behind him. And tagging behind those suitcases like little ducklings were a couple of sandy-haired boys with rumpled clothes and identical faces.

"No," Miranda said again, more firmly this time. "Surely you aren't…"

"Your sister asked me to bring them to you," Jack said, setting the suitcases down and nodding toward the twins. "They aren't any trouble. They're kind of quiet, actually."

Panic was beginning to build in her throat. She swallowed to clear her voice. "I don't understand…"

"Lisa explained everything in her letter. She said you would understand after you read it. And she told me to tell you she's sorry, and she thanks you for helping her. Now, I've got to go. I've got a long trip ahead of me tonight."

"Wait a minute." Miranda moved after him when he turned to walk away. "Where are you going? You aren't just going to leave them here."

Without slowing down, Jack looked over his shoulder. "Sorry, ma'am, but I've got to go. Read the letter from your sister. That'll explain everything."

Openmouthed in disbelief, Miranda watched the man climb behind the wheel of an extended cab pickup truck and drive away without even looking back. Only then did she turn, very slowly, to face the reality of two young, somber faces gazing expectantly up at her.

"Are you our aunt 'Randa?" one of the boys asked in a quavering voice while his twin hovered shyly behind him.

"Yes," she answered in a near groan. "I suppose I am." And heaven help them all, she almost added.

"We'd better get them inside while you read your letter," Mark murmured, breaking into her momentary paralysis. "It's cool out here tonight, and they aren't even wearing jackets over those T-shirts."

"Inside?" Miranda turned to him, feeling as though she were seeing him through a sudden fog. "My apartment?"

Apparently assessing the situation and deciding that someone had to take charge, he reached out his hand. "Give me your key. I'll unlock the door."

She shook her head in an effort to clear her muddled mind. She didn't need anyone taking charge here, she assured herself. She had just needed a moment to recuperate from the shock. "I'll do it."

After opening the door, she reached in to turn on a light, then moved aside and motioned toward the boys. "Come on in. We'll try to straighten this out."

Mark dragged the suitcases in behind him as he entered. Miranda closed the door, then turned to find the twins still staring at her with those huge, unblinking brown eyes. "Uh, do you guys need anything?"

"He's got to pee," one of them said, pointing to the other.

She didn't have a clue which boy was which. They looked so much alike she couldn't imagine anyone being able to tell them apart. Not to mention that they hadn't even been able to talk the last time she'd seen them.

"The bathroom is through there," she said, pointing to the bedroom door. "Um, do you need any help?" If so, she was sending Mark, she decided. He had experience at this sort of thing, even if his kids were girls.

But the boy shook his head, turned and hurried toward the door as if he really couldn't wait a moment longer. His twin continued to stare at Miranda.

"Okay," she said after taking a deep breath. "I need to read this letter. You can go sit on the couch until your brother comes back," she told him.

"I've got to pee, too."

"Then go wait at the bathroom door until he's finished and then you can both sit on the couch until we figure out what's going on. And both of you wash your hands," she called after him when he turned to follow his brother. It seemed like something she should say, since she seemed to be in charge of them at the moment, she thought with a gulp.

"Maybe it would be better if I leave now," Mark suggested, making a slight movement toward the door. "This seems to be family business."

She reached out to grab his sleeve. "Don't you dare," she told him, not even bothering to try to hide her desperation. "You can't just walk away and leave me alone with them."

He hesitated a moment, then nodded. "Read the letter, Miranda. Let's find out what's going on."

She ripped into the envelope, hoping without much optimism that the contents would reveal that Lisa was on her way to pick up her sons. Maybe she had simply been detained for an hour or so, and she had asked her friend to bring the boys ahead for some reason. Lisa probably just needed another loan, and then she—and her twins—would be on their way to the next adventure, leaving Miranda contentedly alone in her tiny apartment and her comfortable, self-centered routines.

But she knew after reading only the first line of the brief letter that nothing would ever be quite the same after this. And she didn't for the life of her know what she was going to do about it.

Chapter Four

Mark could tell by the look on Miranda's face that the letter from her sister did not contain good news. "What does it say?"

Miranda's amber eyes held a stunned expression when she looked up at him. "Lisa has gone into protective custody. She sent the boys to me because she can't take them with her. Or to be more specific, she doesn't *want* to take them. She says she's tired of trying to be a good mother and failing miserably at it."

"Oh, man." The words were a groan as Mark pictured the two cute little boys in the next room who'd been deserted by their mother.

"Mark, she says she can't ever see any of us again—that she knows things that could be detrimental to some very powerful people in the government, so in return for her cooperation and her future silence, she's being given a new identity and a new start in a secret location. She got permission to send the boys to me, but I'm instructed never to try to find her or make contact with her at the risk of getting both her and me into big trouble."

"Damn. What has she gotten herself into?"

"She's pretty vague about it, but it has something to do with…with murder and racketeering. She blamed it all on a man, of course; said he got her into a dangerous situation against her better judgment. As if she *has* any better judgment," she added bitterly. "And as if you can ever believe everything my sister says. She has a habit of wildly embroidering her stories."

He heard the anger and disappointment in her voice, and he couldn't blame her for either. The repercussions of Lisa's poor judgment affected more people than just herself—most notably the two children who had just returned from the other room and now stood gazing somberly at Miranda.

She looked back at the towheaded duo with an expression of near panic. Mark couldn't fault her for that, either. Anyone would be stunned to suddenly become responsible for five-year-old twins who were basically strangers. He would feel pretty much the same way—and he had experience at single parenthood. Miranda must feel completely out of her element.

One of the boys yawned and rubbed his eyes. Poor kids had to be wiped out—not to mention scared and confused. And since Miranda still seemed gripped by the paralysis of shock, someone needed to take charge here, at least until she recovered enough to think clearly.

"My name is Mark," he told the boys. "I'm a friend of your aunt's. What are your names?"

"I'm Kasey," one of the boys replied. "This is Jamie."

Mark tried hard to find any distinguishing feature between them, but as far as he could tell they were identical, right down to their white T-shirts, faded blue jeans and white-and-black sneakers.

"Have you boys had anything to eat?" he asked, earning a startled glance from Miranda—as if it had never occurred to her that children needed to be fed.

"Jack got us hamburgers," the same boy who had spoken before replied. Kasey, Mark reminded himself. Jamie seemed to be the shyer of the two. As long as they remained standing exactly where they were, he knew which was which—but once they moved, he would be completely clueless again.

"Either of you want a drink of water or anything?"

They shook their heads, the movements so perfectly coordinated that Mark had the unsettling feeling he was seeing double. "Okay, then," he said, "we need to find you a place to sleep. You both look tired."

Jamie moved a step closer to his more-confident twin. Reading the body language, Mark assured him, "Don't worry, you can stay close together. Maybe you can both sleep in your aunt's bed for tonight and she can take the couch?"

Slowly coming back to coherence, Miranda nodded. "Yeah, we can do that for tonight." She looked at Mark. "You can stay for a little while longer, can't you? We need to talk after they're in bed."

She obviously needed advice, and since he was the only other adult around at the moment, it looked as though he was elected. Fortunately it wasn't particularly late, since he had brought her straight home after dinner. "I'll call Mrs. McSwaim and tell her I'll be awhile yet. She won't mind. I'm sure my kids are already in bed."

Miranda gave him a wan smile of gratitude, then turned back to her nephews. "So, do you two have pajamas and toothbrushes in those suitcases?"

Two synchronized nods. Mark wondered if the boys were always this quiet, or were simply overwhelmed by being uprooted and left with strangers. He suspected the latter.

Miranda drew a deep breath, and he could see her usual spirit slowly begin to reassert itself. "Okay," she said, "let's get you guys into those pj's."

A short while later, Miranda watched her nephews climb into her bed. It was a queen-size bed, which took up most of the small bedroom, but she liked having plenty of room to stretch out while she slept.

The twins looked even smaller than before as they huddled in the center of the mattress. Considering everything, she supposed they were being brave and stoic about their circumstances, but the pallor of their faces and the expressions in their big brown eyes told her they were extremely shaken.

"Do either of you need anything else?" she asked as she lingered awkwardly beside the bed.

They shook their heads against the pillows.

"Well, then, I'll be in the next room if you need anything. Oh, and this is the only bathroom in the apartment, so don't be alarmed if you hear me moving around in there during the night, okay?"

Two more simultaneous nods.

"Okay." This was so very weird. She took a step toward the door. "Good night."

"Aunt 'Randa?"

The quiet little voice stopped her just as she reached for the light switch. She didn't know who had spoken, but she guessed it was Kasey, since he seemed to do most of the talking for the duo. "Yes?"

"Could you leave the door open?"

Of course they were scared, she thought with a sudden rush of pity. The poor kids were in a strange place with a woman they barely knew. It was mind-boggling to realize that she was all they had at the moment. That she was totally responsible for their welfare.

Swallowing hard, she nodded and turned off the light, then stepped out of the room. She left the door ajar by a good three inches, so the light from the living room would spill into the bedroom, at least until after the boys were asleep.

Mark waited for her at the kitchen table. At her request, he had made a pot of decaffeinated coffee—not that she expected to get any sleep tonight even without the effects of caffeine.

"Did you call your baby-sitter?" she asked as she poured coffee into a mug. Mark already had a steaming cup in front of him.

"Yes. She's my housekeeper. She lives only a couple of doors down from me, so it isn't a problem for me to be a bit late. I'll walk her home."

"It must be convenient for you to have a housekeeper and nanny. Especially one who lives so close by."

"It is. I used to do taxes for her and her husband. When her husband died last year, she didn't want to sell her house, but she was lonely, and she had no family to turn to, so we worked out an arrangement. It has turned out very well for both of us."

He really was a compulsive caregiver, Miranda thought as she took a seat at the little round table. Even when it came to hiring his household help, he was actually providing companionship and a little extra income for a lonely widow.

While taking in strays might be commonplace for Mark, it was hardly characteristic for Miranda. "What am I going to do with these boys?" she asked, hoping he would have a suggestion, since her own mind was pretty much devoid of ideas.

"First you should probably find out whatever you can about your sister's situation."

Miranda handed him her sister's letter, which she had already read twice. "Maybe you should read this."

He seemed a bit reluctant to unfold the page. "You're sure? After all, this is your personal business."

"You're my accountant," she said with a shrug. "There's very little you don't already know about me."

"Financially, maybe. This is different."

"Still, I've always valued your advice, and I would appreciate any you can offer me now."

He hesitated a moment longer, then opened the letter and began to read silently.

Miranda could almost recite the words along with him. Her sister had starkly described the trouble she was in, laying the blame on someone else, and had then begged Miranda to take care of her twins.

It had taken this mess to make Lisa realize what a terrible mother she had been to them, she had written. Selfish and irresponsible and immature. Even if she could take them with her now, they deserved to be raised by someone more settled and responsible, like their aunt Miranda. Lisa needed to put her mistakes behind her—presumably including her twins among those mistakes—and start a new life for herself.

She had packed their birth certificates and immunization records in Kasey's suitcase, she explained. They had been healthy children who rarely needed medical attention, so Miranda needn't worry about that.

"The boys have no one else to turn to," she had added. "Miranda, I know this is a lot to ask of you, but you won't regret it. They're good kids. And they're your family."

Family. Miranda grimaced as she repeated the word

in her mind. It had never been a particularly sentimental concept for her, since her own had been so dysfunctional. The idealized image of loving, supportive parents was foreign to her. The only genuine love she had known as a child had come from her maternal grandmother, who had tried her best to compensate for the emotional neglect her granddaughters had received from their parents.

Her grandmother had died when Miranda was only ten. After that, there had been no one for her to turn to for emotional support except her older sister. And now Lisa had turned to her.

"This doesn't sound good," Mark murmured, refolding the letter.

"No. If she has already disappeared into the witness protection program, there's little chance that I'll ever be able to find her, right?"

"I have a client who's an attorney. I'll ask him to look into this as a favor to me. He owes me a few."

"Thank you. I'd appreciate that. In the meantime, what am I going to do with these kids?"

"You don't have to work tomorrow, do you?"

"No, I wasn't planning to go in at all this weekend."

"That's good. That will give you time to make arrangements."

"What sort of arrangements?"

"You'll have to make plans for some sort of childcare while you're working. And there are steps you need to take to have yourself named their legal guardian. My attorney friend can help you with that part, too.

It's clear from this letter that your sister is voluntarily giving up her parental rights."

"Just wait a minute, Mark." Aware of the partially opened bedroom door, she leaned closer to him, keeping her voice low. "I can't be their legal guardian. Obviously I'm not set up to raise a couple of boys, even if that were something I wanted to take on."

He hesitated a moment, then asked, "What about their father?"

She spread her hands, noting that they were unsteady. "I never even knew his name. And you can bet Lisa won't tell us, even if we manage to find her. She said she promised him she would never contact him after he gave her the financial settlement."

"Is there any way you could send them to your parents?"

She felt her expression harden. "Weren't you paying attention when I told you about them? They won't help. Nor would I ask them to. I'd rather give the kids to strangers than to send them into that cold, rigid, utterly dismal environment."

"They're really that bad?"

"Trust me. My father is a throwback to the Puritans. His word is law, and his laws are unbending. He has very specific ideas about how the world should be run, and about the role of women—which is to be quiet, submissive, dependent and obedient to men."

"And your mother goes along with that?"

"My mother is content to have all her decisions made for her so she can drift along in a safe, comfortable, predictable world of her own. She's borderline agoraphobic and rarely leaves the house. My grandmother said she was always like that—afraid of her own shadow and happiest when she had someone to handle every worrisome problem for her.

"She and my father are the perfect match, I suppose. Lisa and I just happened to inherit more of his nature than our mother's, which didn't please him at all. We weren't content to be dutiful, submissive, undemanding daughters who would live at home until he found proper mates for us, if he ever did. That was what he expected from us, and he was furious that we had other plans. There's no way I would send Lisa's boys into that home to be raised with those twisted values."

"Well, since you've ruled out everyone else, that just leaves you," Mark said quietly. "Or the strangers you mentioned earlier."

"Foster care?" she whispered.

He nodded. "I survived it. I suppose they will, too, if you can't keep them yourself."

For the first time since she had moved in, Miranda's apartment seemed much too small to her. As if the walls were closing in, and all the air was escaping. As if she were caught in a trap. "How can I possibly keep them here? There's barely room for me, much less a couple of kids. I'm not even sure my lease would allow them to live here with me."

"This apartment is too small for them," Mark agreed.

"And there's my job. Sometimes I'm at the office as much as sixty hours a week. I go on business trips three or four times a year. I can't afford a housekeeper and an overnight nanny, even if I had a bed for her to sleep in."

"It would be expensive for you to take them in, though I could help you find a way to swing it financially. It would take most of your earnings, so you'd have very little left to put away in savings, but we could probably stash away a small amount each month."

Her fingers tightened around her cup of untasted coffee. She had worked so hard for her money, equating her slowly building savings with independence and security. It had been so important to her never to be dependent on anyone else again.

"I can't do this, Mark," she murmured miserably. "I'm not qualified to raise a couple of kids. I don't have the resources or the experience or the right personality for the job. It would be unfair to them to leave them with someone so completely clueless about kids."

"Then that brings us back to the only other recourse. Foster care." If there was any disapproval in his voice, Miranda couldn't hear it, nor did she see any criticism in his expression. He seemed to be making an effort to stay completely nonjudgmental about this process, offering his services only as a sounding board for her decision making.

She swallowed hard. "Foster parents are carefully screened, aren't they? Only the best and most caring homes are approved, right?"

"Ideally that would be true, of course. But since there are far more children in need of placement than there are qualified homes for them, it isn't always the case. Still, I'm sure the social workers would find somewhere for Kasey and Jamie to go, even if it took a couple of attempts to find the right setting for them."

She had a sudden mental picture of the boys being continuously uprooted and moved from place to place. She wondered if Mark had deliberately planted that image, despite his outward appearance of careful objectivity. "I can't keep them, Mark."

"You're the only one who can make that decision, of course."

She didn't bother to ask what *he* would do in her situation. She had little doubt that he would simply make room for two more in his life and his household. That was what he did, who he was. A caregiver. Miranda had never aspired to take care of anyone but herself—with the occasional exception of helping out Lisa on a temporary and superficial basis.

"Maybe you should wait until Monday before you call anyone," Mark suggested. "Weekends aren't the best time to try to get help from the Department of Human Services."

Even the thought of being responsible for a couple of five-year-olds for forty-eight hours made her nervous, but she supposed that was the least she could do for them. "All right. I'll wait until Monday. I guess I can take Monday off to make arrangements for the boys. I have some personal days accumulated."

"Mmm."

She gave him a hard look, trying to determine if there

was criticism in the sound he had made, but his expression was still closed to her. "Are there any suggestions you can offer in the meantime? Like what I'm supposed to do with a couple of five-year-olds for an entire weekend?"

"Make sure they eat three well-balanced meals a day. Have them brush their teeth and take their baths. Don't let them play in the traffic or stick their fingers into open light sockets. Belt them into the back seat when you take them out in your car. What else do you need to know?"

She rolled her eyes. "What do I do with them when they *aren't* eating or bathing—or trying to stick their fingers into light sockets?"

"You could take them to the park and let them play on the playground. Take them to a kids' movie—my girls liked the one we saw the other night. Take them to Pizza 'n' Prizes and let them play the games there. There are plenty of things you can do."

The mention of his girls gave her an idea. "Maybe we could all go to the park together? The twins could play with your girls. They would probably have a great time."

"Coward."

"Hey, I'm not denying it. I told you I don't know anything about parenting."

Mark nodded abruptly. "Okay. I don't usually work Saturdays, anyway, once the worst part of tax season is over. We'll take the kids to the park. Why don't we meet at my place at three, after Madison's nap?"

"Sounds good to me." She had a feeling that she and the boys would all be relieved to see other people by then.

She walked him to the door, then put a hand on his arm to detain him when he moved to step through it. "Mark?"

"Yeah?"

"Thank you."

"For the dinner? I enjoyed it."

"So did I, but that isn't what I was talking about. Thank you for helping me deal with all this tonight. I might have panicked when the boys were dumped on my doorstep had I been here alone. You were calm and practical and helpful, and I needed that."

"You're welcome." He surprised her by reaching up to rub his thumb lightly across her lower lip. "Too bad they couldn't have arrived a few minutes later, hmm?"

Remembering the kiss that had been interrupted before it began, she sighed lightly. Too bad, indeed. But now that they would be seeing each other again the next day—strictly as friends, of course—the time for a one-time, curiosity-satisfying kiss had passed.

"Too bad," she agreed with a touch of regret she didn't even try to hide from him. "Good night, Mark."

He dropped his hand and stepped out of the apartment. She closed the door behind him, then looked toward the bedroom and drew a deep, shaky breath. Forty-eight hours, she reminded herself. She could handle this.

She would worry about Monday when it arrived.

* * *

An odd sound woke Miranda from her restless dozing on the living room couch. She lay still for a moment, wondering if she had been dreaming. But then she heard it again, a whimper coming from the bedroom.

She had worn a heavy, oversize T-shirt and dorm pants for sleeping, so she didn't bother reaching for a robe when she tossed the light blanket aside and stood. Pushing her hair out of her face, she moved toward the bedroom.

The sounds were coming from the bed. She turned on the light. "What's wrong?"

The boys were huddled together in the center of the big mattress. One of them was sniffling, his face red and wet with tears. The other boy—Kasey, she would bet—seemed to have been offering comfort.

"Jamie?" she hazarded, moving closer to the bed. "What's the matter? Did you have a bad dream?"

"He misses Mama," Kasey answered for his brother, confirming her guess at their identity.

Miranda's throat tightened. Once again she felt completely helpless, her inexperience with children almost overwhelming her.

She perched on the edge of the bed and started to reach out to Jamie, but then she pulled her hand back, not knowing quite what she had intended to do. "I'm sorry, Jamie. I know you miss your mom. I miss her, too."

It was the truth, actually. Beneath the anger she still

felt over Lisa's foolishness was a deep sadness that her sister had gotten into such a bind.

She had seen Lisa only a handful of times in the past twelve years, but they were still sisters. That connection had not been broken just because they had chosen radically different paths.

She didn't want to promise the boys anything she couldn't deliver, but she would try to contact Lisa somehow, if Mark's client knew how she could do so. Surely Lisa had known how ill-equipped Miranda was to deal with them.

"Mama said we're going to live with you now," Kasey said.

"Well, uh…" She patted the pillow behind Jamie. "Why don't you lie back down and try to get some sleep?"

"Sometimes when we couldn't sleep, Mama would stay with us," Kasey said, his little voice rising at the end to turn the sentence into a question.

"Oh." She moistened her lips, then looked at Jamie, whose eyes were still swimming in tears. She knew she wasn't offering him much comfort, since she didn't have the first clue what that entailed. "Okay, I guess I can stay awhile. Would that help, Jamie?"

He studied her face a moment, then slowly nodded. It occurred to her that she had never actually heard his voice, but this didn't seem to be the right time to push him to speak.

It took a bit of squirming and straightening, but a few minutes later the light had been turned off and Miranda lay in the center of the bed between the boys. She had expected simply to lie on one side of the bed and tiptoe out of the room when they were asleep again, but Kasey had instructed her to get in the middle. That was what their mother always did when they had trouble sleeping and were allowed to crawl into her bed, he had added.

Resisting an impulse to point out the very obvious fact that she was not their mother, she complied with Kasey's instructions.

Now she lay flat on her back staring at the darkened ceiling and wondering if she would be able to sleep a wink during the five hours that remained until dawn. She could already tell that Kasey was a wiggler, rooting into his pillow like a newborn puppy. Lying on his side facing her, Jamie hadn't moved or made a sound since she had turned out the light and crawled in between the boys.

She worried about that one. He seemed so vulnerable—both the twins did, actually, but especially Jamie. She tried to remember if he had been so subdued the last time she'd seen him, but that had been almost three years ago, and it had been a very brief visit.

She had speculated recently that her nephews were probably wild little brats, since Lisa had made such a big deal out of her no-rules, no-roots, all-fun-all-the-time lifestyle. Instead the boys seemed to be even more restrained than Lisa and Miranda had been in their rigid and restrictive childhood home.

Very weird, she thought with a slight shake of her

head against her pillow. And only another indication of how little she knew about children.

She was definitely out of her league here. She didn't even know how to comfort a kid who had woken up crying for his mother. She was sure the boys would be better off in a qualified foster home with people who had been trained to deal with children in domestic crisis situations.

Just as that thought crossed her mind, Jamie moved closer to her and nestled his cheek against her upper arm. He gave a long, poignant sigh and then slipped into sleep, his breathing slow and even.

Afraid to move—and wondering why she suddenly felt as though both boys were lying directly on her chest, making it hard for her to breathe—Miranda lay motionless and tried to will herself to sleep. She was suddenly very anxious for morning to arrive.

Chapter Five

Mark half expected Miranda to look frazzled and exhausted when she arrived at his house Saturday afternoon. It was a clear day, unseasonably warm for late April. He figured that once the twins had rested, they'd have recovered the typical energy of five-year-old boys. He imagined they had been all but bouncing off the walls of Miranda's miniscule apartment.

Instead he opened the door to find Miranda looking as fresh and pretty as ever in a yellow and green striped boat-neck T-shirt, khaki cargo pants, backless sandals and her characteristic gold hoop earrings. Her usual inch of abdomen was showing, and he had to make an effort not to glance in that direction when he greeted her.

"How's it been going?" he asked.

She made a slightly quizzical face and motioned toward the boys who stood silently behind her, neat and clean in matching dark red T-shirts, blue jeans and sneakers. "As you can see, everything's fine."

"Are they here yet, Daddy?" Payton barreled down the wood-floored hallway, her sneakers skidding when she came to a stop behind him. Never one to meet a stranger, she smiled broadly in welcome to the twins. "Hi. I'm Payton. You want to see my room?"

The boys looked up at Miranda. She nodded to them. "Go ahead."

Mark ushered the trio of visitors into the house and closed the door behind them. Payton was already motioning the boys toward the stairs. "I got a new toy and it makes animal noises when you push the buttons. It's fun."

The twins obligingly followed her up the stairs. One of the boys kept looking over his shoulder at Miranda, as if he were afraid she would leave while she was out of his sight. She gave him a cheery thumbs-up, and he allowed himself to be towed along in Payton's wake.

"Would you like some iced tea? Or coffee?" Mark offered.

Miranda turned away from the staircase. "No, thanks. The boys and I had a late lunch, and I'm still full."

He led her into the den and motioned toward a chair. "Have a seat. It'll take a while for Payton to show the twins every toy she owns. They'll let us know when they want to go to the park."

She glanced around the pine-walled room filled with comfortably overstuffed furniture. This was the room Mark usually hung out in when he wasn't working, where he sat with his newspapers and books or watched TV. It was decorated more for relaxation than style, but he liked the earthy colors and welcoming atmosphere.

Poochie lay curled on the hearthrug like the final accessory in the homey decor. He looked up when Mark and Miranda entered, then yawned and went back to sleep. He and Payton had played out in the backyard all morning, and the dog's energy had given out before the child's.

"Hi, pup," Miranda said. "I didn't know you had a dog."

"He was a stray."

Miranda settled into a forest-green recliner. "This is a nice room."

Mark took a seat on the green-and-burgundy plaid couch. "Thanks. This has always been my favorite room."

"You have a nice home. It must be very convenient to have your office attached."

"It is. I was lucky to find this house in a neighborhood that permitted a home-based office. That room was originally a dining room, but I changed some big windows into an entrance and added a wall to make a reception area. The kitchen has a nook attached that holds a round table big enough for six, so I didn't see any need for a formal dining room."

"It's great." Miranda clasped her fingers in her lap,

looking uncharacteristically self-conscious now that
they had exhausted the subject of his house.

"Are you sure I can't get you anything to drink?"

"No, I'm fine, thanks. Where's your other daughter?"

"Madison's upstairs with Mrs. McSwaim. She was
taking a nap, but I'm sure she's with Payton and the
twins by now. Maddie's a bit shy around strangers, but
Payton has a way of drawing her into the activities."

"When it comes to shyness, she has serious compe-
tition from Jamie."

"He still hasn't opened up?"

He watched a worried expression cross Miranda's
face. "No. He hasn't said a word since he arrived at my
apartment last night. Not to me, anyway."

"It had to be an upsetting experience for him, being
taken from his mother."

"I realize that, but he seems to be unusually with-
drawn and anxious. He's never more than a half step
from Kasey, who does all the talking for both of them.
Maybe Jamie needs counseling or something."

"I'm sure he just needs to feel safe and settled. Kids
crave routines and boundaries, you know. From what
you've told me, they haven't had much of that in their
lives."

"Lisa has been their only constant—other than each
other, of course."

"Exactly. And now she's gone, so it's only natural
Jamie would cling even more tightly to his brother.
And since he isn't sure how long you'll be in his life,

he's probably a bit reluctant to become too attached to you."

"I suppose you're right."

He noticed that she still looked concerned. No matter what she said, Miranda felt a connection to her nephews, if only a tenuous one. Mark still found it hard to believe she intended simply to hand them over to a social worker on Monday. That was why he had talked her into waiting until the weekend was over. He hoped by then she would overcome her initial panic and rethink that decision.

He certainly understood her quandary. She was content with her life the way it was, with no one to be responsible for except herself. She was doing well in her job, happy in her little apartment, comfortable with the savings she had slowly accumulated.

Finding herself suddenly saddled with her five-year-old nephews changed everything. She now faced more responsibility than she had ever imagined, and her first instinctive response was to push that burden onto someone else.

A perfectly reasonable knee-jerk reaction, but Mark thought she would be making a mistake not to at least try to make a home for her unfortunate nephews. After all, they were family. And they needed her.

"DHS will probably arrange for counseling for the boys, don't you think?" she asked him, still fretting about Jamie's problems. "I assume that any child whose parent suddenly disappears from his life needs help adjusting."

"They'll get counseling. Maybe. Eventually. You know how the child welfare system is—always backed up. The worse cases have to be treated first, and Jamie won't exactly be high priority, unless he suddenly starts acting out and causing problems in his foster setting."

Her throat worked with a hard swallow. "You said you were happy in your last foster home, right?"

"I said I was relatively content there because I liked my foster family. Still, there wasn't a day that went by that I didn't miss my mother and my sister."

Her fingers twisted more tightly in her lap. "Was your sister's foster care experience a positive one?"

"To this day Terry refuses to talk about the year she spent in foster care. The only thing she'll say is that she spent the entire time wanting desperately to go home."

New lines of stress appeared around Miranda's mouth. "Kasey and Jamie will miss their mother wherever they are. Despite Lisa's mistakes, they love her."

"Of course they do."

"It will be good for them to be placed in a nice home with two parents and a steady, regular routine."

"Yes, I suppose that would be ideal."

"You don't sound very confident that they'll get an environment like that."

"Yes, well, I'm probably a bit biased by my own experience with foster care. It took three attempts before I found a place where I would even stay without trying to run away every few days."

Miranda thought about that for a moment, then asked, "Do you think the social workers will let me meet potential foster families and choose a place for the boys?"

"No, Miranda, that won't happen. Once you turn them over to the state, you'll have no further say in what becomes of them."

She shot him a look that seemed almost angry. "You're *trying* to worry me, aren't you?"

Mark spread his hands. "I'm merely trying to answer your questions honestly. And from the perspective of my own experiences."

"I can't keep them, Mark. I'm no more qualified than any of the foster parents you stayed with unsuccessfully."

"I wouldn't say that. You're their aunt. And you obviously care about them, or you wouldn't be so worried about what's going to happen to them."

"Well, of course I care what happens to them," she responded irritably. "I'd be pretty heartless not even to worry at all about them, wouldn't I?"

"I never said you were heartless," he answered gently. "Just the opposite, in fact. You want the best for your nephews, and you're afraid you can't provide that for them."

She sighed deeply and looked down at her clenched hands. "Now you're making me sound too noble. You're fully aware that there's a part of me that simply doesn't want to take on the responsibilities involved with the boys. I'm selfish enough to want to keep my life the way it has been."

"Also perfectly natural," he assured her. "Anyone

would feel the same way. What your sister did has turned a lot of lives upside down."

Miranda gazed broodingly at the once-stray dog snoozing on the rug. "You wouldn't hesitate to take them in if they were your sister's kids, would you? You'd simply make room for them in your home and in your life. You wouldn't even think twice about it."

"Are you kidding? The thought of trying to raise four kids on my own, in addition to running my business, is enough to make me break out in hives. As it is, I hardly have a life of my own. Don't you think there are times when I'd like to chuck everything and escape to Tahiti for a life of sand and rum and women in bikinis? Trust me, that's a daydream I turn to fairly often when my life gets hectic and I wonder how I ended up a single-dad accountant at only thirty."

She seemed a bit startled by his candid response. "But you would take them in, wouldn't you?"

"Of course," he answered simply. "It wouldn't be a decision I would make lightly or without a few regrets, but I couldn't give my nephews over to strangers. This isn't a judgment against any decision you make for yourself, Miranda. I'm simply answering your question about what I would do."

She was silent a few minutes, then said, "Do you mind if I ask you a personal question?"

Since he had become privy to an important aspect of her family life, he supposed it was only fair that she should ask a few questions about him. "Go ahead."

"What happened to your wife? Did she die?"

"No. She left. Brooke is the kind of woman who is never truly satisfied with her life. She always believes the next big change will bring happiness. She wanted to get married, so we got married. She wanted a child, so we had a child—and then another. The next thing she decided was that she needed to be single and unencumbered to truly experience life. So she took off."

"You mean she just walked away from her kids?" Miranda seemed truly shocked.

"Yes." It still stung to have to admit that he had been so oblivious to Brooke's true character. He had been taken in by her beautiful face, her passionate nature, and her claim to need him desperately.

By the time she had finally left, he'd understood that he had married a woman who had no ability to truly connect with anyone. She said all the right things, but she had no concept of what the words really meant. Love. Commitment. Even motherhood.

Apparently Brooke had a few things in common with Miranda's sister. Mark couldn't help wondering if Miranda was a bit like them, especially since she was already planning how best to rid herself of the responsibility of her sister's twins.

Maybe he was being unfair—heck, he knew he was—but when it came to kids, he had a very prominent soft spot. He couldn't imagine how anyone could walk away from children who depended on them, but maybe that was just him.

"How long has she been gone?"

"Two years. Madison was just a baby."

"And she hasn't seen them since?"

"No. She said she would come last Christmas, but she had the chance to go to Europe with a singer she met somewhere, so she chose that, instead." And she had seemed surprised when she'd called that Mark had even questioned her choice.

Who would turn down a chance to tour Europe with a band? she had asked in genuine bewilderment. She had implied that going to Europe was a once-in-a-life-time opportunity, while she could see her children any-time. Not that she had bothered.

Miranda shook her head, her forehead creased with a scowl. "Why do people have children and then screw them up for life? My parents never should have had kids. Lisa obviously wasn't thinking about her boys when she chose to live on the edge. And your ex left you with two little girls to raise on your own. I know you're doing a great job, but they'll certainly have bag-gage to carry as a result of her desertion."

"I'm sure they will," Mark muttered. He had been all too aware of that inevitability since the day Brooke had taken off, leaving her children crying for her.

"Now you know why I've made a point not to have kids."

He lifted an eyebrow. "Because you're afraid of 'screwing them up'? Or because you didn't want to take on the responsibility?"

"Both."

He glanced at the framed photographs on the man-tel. His girls. When he spoke, his voice had softened.

"I've talked about the duties, but maybe I haven't talked enough about the rewards. My kids are the greatest thing that ever happened to me. For every sacrifice I've made for them, I've been repaid beyond measure. I wouldn't trade my time with them for any amount of wealth or adventure or selfish pleasure. I've never pursued any more worthwhile goal than raising them to be productive and admirable adults."

He felt a bit self-conscious when he finished that impassioned monologue, hoping he hadn't sounded too self-righteous. But he had meant every word he'd said.

Before Miranda could respond, the room was invaded by children. One of the twins burst in first. Mark caught just a glimpse of tear-dampened cheeks before the boy leaped into Miranda's lap and buried his face in her shoulder.

Startled to find her arms suddenly full with a distraught boy, Miranda patted him awkwardly and asked, "What's wrong, Jamie?"

It didn't take a big leap to figure out which twin she held, since she had learned early that Jamie was the one most likely to burst into tears and seek comfort.

Standing nearby, Kasey and Payton both erupted into noisy explanations that jumbled together and almost drowned each other out.

"She said our mother…"

"All I said was…"

"…was never coming…"

"…*my* mama didn't come…"

"...and Jamie got upset..."

"...he started crying for *no* reason..."

"...and I said..."

"Just wait a minute," Mark cut in sharply, holding up a hand. "One at a time. Kasey, you go first. What's wrong with your brother?"

While Payton hopped in impatience to speak and Madison climbed into her father's lap, Kasey embarked on a lengthy and roundabout explanation. Settling Madison on his knee, Mark seemed to follow the tale with less difficulty than Miranda—probably from experience.

Apparently Kasey had told Payton that he and Jamie were staying with their aunt while their mother was away for a while. Payton had then informed the twins that their mother would never come back, at which point Jamie had gotten upset.

"Why did you tell them that?" Mark asked his daughter when Kasey stopped for breath.

"I just said maybe we could all be friends and stuff 'cause they'll be living with their aunt all the time now," she replied ingenuously.

"You said our mother won't ever come back," Kasey accused her as Jamie sniffled in agreement.

"Well, she won't," Payton shot back. "Mamas don't come back when they leave, do they, Daddy?"

Mark looked tempted to groan, but he kept his voice even when he replied, "Kasey and Jamie's mother had to go away, Payton, but that doesn't mean they'll never see her again."

"We don't ever see *our* mama," Payton argued matter-of-factly, motioning to include her little sister in the statement.

Miranda saw what might have been chagrin in Mark's eyes before he replied, "That doesn't mean you won't ever see her again. And it doesn't have anything to do with Jamie and Kasey."

Miranda couldn't help wondering how Mark really felt about his ex-wife now. He had spoken of her with little emotion earlier, as if he had few feelings left for her at all, but how would he really respond if she suddenly appeared on his doorstep again? As committed as he was to family and responsibility, would he feel obligated to take her back?

As she studied handsome Mark Wallace and his two beautiful daughters in their comfortable home, she wondered what his ex-wife had been thinking to leave all this behind. Maybe Miranda had been careful to avoid such domestic entanglements, herself, but she couldn't imagine running out on such a nice family if she had found herself a part of one.

Deciding a change of subject would be advantageous for everyone, she shifted Jamie's head out of her shoulder and pointed toward the hearthrug. "Did you see the dog, Jamie? He looks like a friendly guy, doesn't he?"

The smallish, brown mutt had awakened from his nap when the children had come in. He sat up now watching them with a goofy doggy grin and a wagging tail, seeming to be waiting patiently for someone to notice him.

Kasey hadn't seen the dog until Miranda pointed him out. His face lit up. "A dog! Can we pet him?"

"Of course you can," Mark assured him. "He loves to be petted."

Kasey moved toward the mutt, who wiggled excitedly around the boy's feet. Kasey laughed when the pup licked his chin. "Jamie, come pet him. He's so soft."

Her manner somewhat territorial, Payton knelt to keep one hand on her pet. "His name is Poochie. He's my dog."

"Let the boys play with him, too," Mark instructed her, a note of warning in his voice.

Jamie slid slowly off Miranda's lap, his gaze focused on the dog. She watched as he crossed the room, then knelt beside the dog. Cautiously he stuck out a hand and touched Poochie's back. Tail wagging frantically, Poochie squirmed around to lick Jamie's fingers.

Jamie giggled. The dog reached up to lick the boy's still-damp cheek, and the giggle turned into a breathy laugh.

Unconsciously holding her breath, Miranda looked at Mark. He smiled back at her over Madison's head.

Miranda was the one who looked away, drawing an unsteady breath. She wasn't sure whether she was more shaken by Jamie's touching response to the little dog, or by that fleeting moment when she had found herself lost in Mark's smiling gray eyes.

Chapter Six

They took Poochie to the park with them. Miranda held the dog's leash while Mark supervised the children on the playground equipment. Jamie clung to Miranda for a few minutes when they first arrived, apparently intimidated by the number of children taking advantage of the warm spring weather, but Miranda shooed him off to play with Kasey and Payton.

Now she sat on a park bench, watching as Jamie followed his brother up the ladder of a slide and pondering the realization that Jamie was starting to form an attachment to her, using her as a substitute for his mother.

She was surprised that he had turned to her so quickly; after all, he hardly knew her. They had spent only a half day together—and a night, she reminded herself with a wince, since her neck was still sore from sleeping in an awkward position.

Just the fact that she was his aunt—and looked quite a bit like his mother—must have been enough to make him see her as someone who would take care of him. She couldn't help wondering how traumatic it would be for him to have yet another adult he had come to depend upon choose to send him away.

Having explored as far as the leash would allow him to go, Poochie hopped up on the bench beside Miranda and butted his head against her in a shameless request to be petted. She sighed lightly and scratched his shaggy ears. "Even you want something from me," she murmured, making his feathery tail pump the air.

She looked from the dog to the slide, where Mark was holding his hands out to Madison as she slid down to him, squealing with delight. The guy was a natural at the daddy thing. Parenthood seemed to come so effortlessly to him—which was probably why he didn't entirely understand her own reluctance to take on the role, no matter what he said to the contrary.

She watched him catch his youngest daughter at the bottom of the slide. Little Madison obviously adored him. There was such absolute trust in her face when she landed in his waiting arms.

Payton was at that self-centered, queen-of-the-world stage where she took his attention for granted. She was as possessive of her father as she had been with her dog, making sure the twins didn't get too much of his time.

Yet he still managed to give attention to the boys, teasing and encouraging Kasey and being gently supportive of Jamie in trying new playground challenges.

Her own father would have considered a playground visit a waste of his valuable time. His daughters were expected to entertain themselves, preferably with instructive and character-building pursuits such as studying and piano practice. Miranda considered him a throwback to Victorian times, when the man had served as the distant and undisputed head of his household, whose only responsibility to his offspring was to provide financial support and firm instruction.

Mark, she realized, watching him toss Madison in the air and catch her, then give giggle-inducing neck nuzzles, was a very different sort of father. Had Stewart Martin been more like him, Lisa and Miranda might have turned out very differently.

Especially Lisa, Miranda added regretfully. Never satisfied with her own accomplishments, Lisa had sought affirmation from too many outside sources. That craving for approval had made her too susceptible to unsavory influences, too easily led into trouble.

Why couldn't Lisa have been satisfied with the love of her children? Why hadn't being a good mother to them been enough of a challenge for her? Miranda shook her head with a renewed sense of frustration and anger.

Her attention returned to the present when a tow-headed boy climbed onto the bench next to her, sitting so close their thighs almost touched. "Jamie?"

He nodded.

"You don't want to play with the others?"

He shook his head.

"Are you getting tired?" she asked, studying the faint purple smudges under his eyes. He hadn't slept very deeply the night before.

Another nod.

Wondering if the boy was ever going to speak to her, Miranda decided not to push him. Instead she shifted the dog closer to Jamie's reach. "Why don't you pet Poochie? He loves having his ears scratched."

Jamie reached out a hand, a slight smile playing on his lips when the dog grinned goofily at him and licked his fingers. Miranda sat back and let Poochie work his magic. Her head was beginning to ache a bit, probably from a combination of weariness, bewilderment and worry.

Thank goodness Mark had coincidentally been with her when the boys had arrived, she thought for at least the dozenth time. Even though she assured herself she could have handled everything on her own, his assistance had certainly come in handy.

It was just after five when the children decided they had had enough of the playground. "I'm hungry," Payton proclaimed.

"Me, too," Kasey seconded, looking up at Miranda.

Having spent the past half hour dozing on the bench with his cheek on Miranda's leg, Jamie rubbed his eyes and nodded agreement.

"Why don't we go out for pizza?" Mark suggested.

"Pizza!" Madison exclaimed, her smudged little face lighting up.

Mark looked at Miranda with an inquiringly lifted eyebrow. She debated maybe a half second before nodding. "Pizza sounds good to me. But what do we do with Poochie?"

Mark made a shooing motion toward the parking lot. "We'll drop him off at home on the way."

Shamelessly taking advantage of another opportunity to avoid being alone with her nephews, Miranda followed the crowd.

It was inevitable, of course, that the time would finally arrive for Miranda to take the boys back to her apartment. Parked in Mark's driveway, she made sure they were belted into the back seat of her car, then walked around to the driver's side, where Mark waited to see her off. His daughters were inside with the housekeeper, giving them their first moment in several hours to speak privately.

"Are you going to be okay with them tonight?" Mark asked. "Do you need anything?"

She shook her head. "Now that they've been fed and entertained, I'm sure everything will be fine. Maybe the boys will be so tired tonight they'll go right to sleep."

"I hope so."

"Thanks for everything this afternoon, Mark. I know you had more important things to do than to help me baby-sit my nephews."

"I had other things I could have done, but nothing more important," he corrected her with a smile.

She tucked a strand of hair behind her ear. "You always say just the right thing, don't you? It must be a talent. I'm afraid it's not one of mine."

He frowned as if he weren't sure whether he had just been complimented or insulted. "Because I don't know the right response to that, I'll simply say goodnight."

She opened her car door and climbed in. "Good night, Mark."

"I'll call you tomorrow, okay? I'd like to know how things are going. And, uh, what you've decided to do about…you know," he added with a glance at the boys.

Her fingers clenched a bit spasmodically on the steering wheel. "You can call, if you like—but nothing has changed about my plans."

"I'll call, anyway," he said, and stepped back to allow her to close the car door.

Miranda sent the twins straight to the bathtub when they arrived at her apartment. Kasey assured her they were quite capable of bathing themselves and washing their own hair, something they had apparently been doing for some time. Relieved, she checked her answering machine while they were splashing around in the bathroom.

There were several messages from various friends, all wondering where she had been this weekend. Three nights had passed now since anyone had seen her out at the clubs, and they wondered where she was keeping herself.

Brandi was convinced Miranda was involved in a

passionate new love affair, and she wanted details. Juicy ones. Oliver was having a cocktail party at his place the next evening, and he wanted Miranda to be sure to attend. "Feel free to bring a friend or two," he'd added casually, being of the-more-the-merrier persuasion.

With a rueful smile, Miranda wondered how Oliver would feel if she brought a couple of five-year-olds to the party. Since most of her friends had much the same attitude about children that Miranda had, it wasn't much of a stretch to conclude that Oliver would be horrified.

It occurred to her only then that none of her current friends had children. Once members of her loose circle married and started families, they tended to disappear. She supposed it was because there wasn't as much time to party once the babies arrived.

Just as she wouldn't be going to Oliver's get-together tomorrow because she had to take care of her nephews. She'd always known that kids would seriously cramp her lifestyle—was it any wonder she had always avoided them so assiduously?

After the boys had bathed, dressed in pajamas and brushed their teeth, she tucked them into her bed again. "I'm going to sleep on the couch tonight," she told them as she hovered by the light switch. "You both know you're safe here, and that I won't let anything happen to you, so we can all sleep easily, okay?"

Two blond heads nodded against the pillows.

Seeing a look of anxiety on the face she assumed was Jamie's, she added gently, "If you need anything, I'm only a few feet away. I'll close the door now, so you won't be disturbed if I watch the news on TV or something, but I'll be able to hear you if you call out to me, okay?"

Jamie looked just a bit more at ease when he nodded again. Feeling an imaginary weight of responsibility lying heavily on her shoulders, Miranda turned off the light and closed the bedroom door.

It was just after 9:00 p.m., which was hours earlier than she usually turned in on a Saturday night. Aware of the need to be quiet, she moved to the couch and picked up a mystery novel she'd started a few weeks earlier, but had lost interest in before she'd made it halfway through.

For nearly an hour she sat there with the book open in her lap, an untouched soda on the table beside her and her feet propped comfortably on the coffee table in front of her. She didn't read a word during that entire time. She was lost in a mental slide show featuring Mark Wallace—images of him sitting at his desk poring over her tax forms, smiling at her over a candlelit dinner table, playing with the children at the park, speaking so kindly to Jamie. The way his face had looked when he was just about to kiss her last night.

What would have happened then had Jack Parsons not shown up with her nephews? Would the kiss have flared into spontaneous passion? Would she have invited him in—and would he have accepted if she had? And if they had carried the kiss into the bedroom, would the results have been as spectacular as she suspected?

Even though she knew it would have been no more

than a brief fling, maybe only the single night, and even though she had never been one to indulge in one-night stands, which were more her sister's style, just this one time she might have made an exception. If for no other reason than to rid herself of the embarrassing crush she had unreasonably developed for the man. She figured it was just a fleeting thing, a combination of lust and curiosity and admiration.

A brief infatuation, she assured herself. She didn't even want it to develop into anything more, considering her aversion to commitment and his ready-made family. But that one night might have been a pleasant aberration, leaving memories she could have savored for a lifetime.

Once again Miranda was awakened not long after she went to sleep, this time by a hand on her shoulder, followed by a tentative voice saying, "Aunt 'Randa? Are you asleep?"

She opened her eyes just as a booming clap of thunder rattled the apartment windows. Only then did she realize that a spring storm was raging outside, complete with thunder, lightning and torrential rain. She had been so soundly asleep, she hadn't even roused, proving how tired she had been when she had finally dropped off to sleep.

"Aunt 'Randa," the boy said again, giving her shoulder another little shake. "Are you awake?"

"I am now." She yawned and sat up. "What's wrong, Kasey? Are you afraid of the storm?"

"I'm Jamie. And I'm a little afraid of the storm, but that's not why I woke you up."

Startled, she studied his face in the bright flash of lightning that momentarily lit the room. "Oh, sorry. I thought you must be…"

Jamie had talked to her. The relief of it made her pause a moment to collect herself before she asked, "Why did you wake me?"

"Kasey's sick. He threw up in the bathroom."

"Oh, cripes." After tossing her blanket aside, Miranda jumped to her feet and ran into the other room.

Kasey was still in the bathroom, his face so pale that the slight smattering of freckles across his cheekbones stood out in stark contrast. Wrinkling her nose at the smell in the room, Miranda opened a cabinet to pull out a washcloth and a can of air freshener. She squirted a bit of the scent before holding the cloth beneath a stream of cool water.

"Sit on the toilet seat," she instructed Kasey, and when he did, she pressed the cloth to his face. "Are you still feeling sick?"

"I don't think so." But he didn't sound entirely confident.

She felt his forehead. A bit clammy, but she didn't think he had a fever. She knew absolutely nothing about childhood illnesses, so she didn't even know what questions she should ask. She settled for, "Do you hurt anywhere?"

Looking miserable and embarrassed, Kasey shook his head. "I'm okay."

"He always throws up when he eats pepperoni pizza," Jamie volunteered.

Still a little startled to hear him speaking, Miranda nodded at him before looking at Kasey again. "Pepperoni always makes you sick, Kasey?"

He nodded.

"Then why did you eat it?"

"Everyone else did."

Which meant either he hadn't wanted to single himself out or he had been reluctant to cause any inconvenience. Maybe he just liked pepperoni pizza and had hoped he would get lucky tonight.

Miranda sighed. "What usually happens after you get sick?"

He shrugged. "I feel better."

So perhaps there was no need to rush him to the closest hospital, after all. She had him brush his teeth, then gave him a glass of water and tucked him back into bed with his brother. "Call out if you need anything, okay? The door will be open."

Kasey nestled into the pillows and she was relieved to see that the color had almost fully returned to his face. "I'll be okay. G'night."

"Good night, Kasey."

Jamie yawned hugely and pulled the covers to his ears. "'Night, Aunt 'Randa."

For some reason she had to swallow a lump in her throat before she could answer, "Good night, Jamie."

Though Mark had told Miranda he would call her on Sunday, he found himself driving into her apartment complex parking lot, instead. He had left the girls with his housekeeper on this rainy afternoon, Madison taking a nap and Payton helping Mrs. McSwaim make cookies.

He probably should have just called, but for some reason he wanted to watch Miranda's face when she told him she was still planning to send her nephews away.

He could still see her sitting on that park bench with the April sun gleaming in her highlighted hair, his dog curled against her left side and Jamie's head resting on her right knee. A soft smile had played on her lips as she'd glanced down at the sleeping boy, and she had looked more relaxed than he had ever seen her.

He didn't try to delude himself that Miranda was secretly harboring a desire for maternal domesticity. He knew she enjoyed her carefree, spur-of-the-moment life, having her evenings open for whatever spontaneous diversion arose. He doubted that a couple of hours at the playground or the pizza parlor had convinced her to swap that freedom for baby-sitters and PTA meetings.

Her car was parked in its space, so she hadn't taken the boys anywhere. He wondered how the three of them were getting along in that tiny apartment.

The smell of popcorn wafted through the doorway when Miranda answered his knock. She was dressed for a casual afternoon in a skimpy peach-colored T-shirt and low-slung faded jeans. Her feet were bare. Her toenails were painted a mango color just a couple of shades darker than her shirt.

He tried to convince himself it was the smell of the popcorn that had him suddenly salivating.

Swallowing hard, he shoved his hands into the pockets of the khaki pants he wore with a dark blue polo shirt. "Sorry for the unannounced visit. It was an impulse."

Her eyebrows rose as a teasing smile curved her lips and brought out the dimple that always drove him crazy. "*You* did something on impulse? Should I mark this on my calendar?"

"Make a note in your diary tonight. 'Mark Wallace graced me with his presence today.'"

Her grin broadened. "Should I draw a heart around your name?"

"That's a given, of course." He hadn't flirted with a woman like this in a long time. He was well aware that the light tone was a cover for much stronger emotions, at least on his part.

Miranda stepped aside. "Come in."

He smiled at the boys sitting on the floor around the coffee table with a board game obviously in progress in front of them. "What are you playing?"

"Trouble," one of the twins replied. Mark assumed it was Kasey. "Aunt 'Randa keeps landing on our pieces and making us go back to start."

Mark chuckled. "She's vicious, huh?"

The other boy nodded. "She said if you're gonna play with her, you better be ready to lose."

"Did she now? She sounds—" Mark faltered as he realized what had just happened, but he recovered quickly to finish "—pretty tough."

He glanced quizzically at Miranda while both boys nodded fervently. When had Jamie started talking? What magic had she performed on him to have the boy looking so confident and content that now Mark couldn't tell one twin from the other?

She gave a barely perceptible shrug before saying, "That's right. When it comes to playing with me, sissies and crybabies need not apply."

"Don't let me keep you from finishing your game."

"That's okay. We'll play some more later." Miranda glanced at the twins. "Why don't you guys go watch the cartoon channel on the TV in my bedroom while I talk to Mr. Wallace?"

After Jamie and Kasey moved obediently into the other room, Miranda turned back to Mark. "Can I get you anything? Coffee? Soda?"

"Coffee sounds good," he replied, running a hand through his rain-dampened hair. "If it's not too much trouble."

"Of course not." She moved around the bar that separated the eat-in kitchen from the living room. "Make yourself comfortable."

He straddled one of the two tall bar stools and leaned his elbows on the wood-grain bar top to watch her make the coffee. "Looks like things are running smoothly here."

"For the most part," she agreed. "It's pretty tight quarters for three, so getting everyone ready in the morning is a challenge."

"When did Jamie start talking?"

"Last night. Kasey was sick, and Jamie came to get me."

Mark frowned. "Kasey was sick?"

"Apparently, pepperoni pizza always does that to him."

"Why didn't he tell us?"

"He didn't want to be difficult."

Mark took a moment to think about that explanation. "That sounds a little sad—that he would rather risk being sick than to make any waves."

Miranda's expression was somber as she pulled two mugs from a cabinet. "I know."

He wondered how to phrase his next remark so as not to sound too judgmental. "As well-behaved and undemanding as your nephews are, it makes me wonder why they feel so compelled to please everyone."

Miranda looked at him from across the bar. "It isn't because Lisa mistreated them in any way. Remember, she and I were subjected to harsh discipline. She would never treat her boys that way—in fact, she probably carried her parenting to the other extreme."

"Probably."

Miranda hesitated, and then sighed. "I've been a bit concerned about the twins' behavior, too. I tried to ask a few questions this morning about their relationship with Lisa. Talking about her made them both sad, but I got the impression the parent-child dynamics were sort of reversed for them. They seemed to feel a responsibility to take care of their mother, to keep her happy. Whenever they misbehaved, she cried and said she was a terrible mother, making them feel miserable and guilty. They both seem to believe it was their fault that she's in trouble now—that they should have been able to stop it somehow."

Mark grimaced.

Taking the expression as an unspoken comment, Miranda nodded. "I'm more convinced than ever that they need counseling to help them deal with this. Even though Jamie's talking again, that doesn't mean he's completely okay emotionally."

"No. He—they both need reassurance. Unconditional love. Security." He paused, then added, "A sense of family."

She almost overfilled a coffee mug. She ripped a paper towel from its holder to wipe up the few drops that had spilled. "Don't start with me again, Wallace."

He continued to watch her steadily. "They're growing very fond of you, Miranda. It's obvious from the way they've responded to you. Maybe because they know you're their aunt, or maybe you just have a way with them, but they're becoming attached to you. It's going to be very difficult for them to be uprooted again."

She was shaking her head before he finished speaking. "You're trying to make me feel guilty now—and trust me, it's working. If things were different—if I had a bigger place and someone to depend on when I'm working or traveling with my job—maybe I would try to take them in, even though I'm hardly qualified to do so. But as it is, it just wouldn't work."

"Maybe if you—"

"Mark, I can't keep them," she snapped, her facial muscles tensed with emotion. "First thing tomorrow I'm calling the Department of Human Services and asking someone to find a foster home for them."

A small, choked sound from the direction of the bedroom made both of them whirl around. Mark was chagrined to see the twins standing there staring at them with huge, stricken eyes.

He should never have started this conversation, he berated himself angrily.

Now look what he had done.

Chapter Seven

"We can't stay with you, Aunt 'Randa?" one of the boys asked in a small voice. Miranda couldn't identify which one had spoken, since they looked equally upset.

Darn Mark for this. Sure, she would have had to talk to the boys soon, but she had hoped to do so at her own pace, after she had decided what to say.

She drew a deep breath. "Sit down, boys. We need to talk."

Looking apologetic, Mark started to rise. "Maybe I should go."

She pointed a finger at him. "You sit, too."

He had started this, so he could darned well stay around and help her deal with it, she thought.

Wisely, Mark didn't attempt to argue with her. He sat.

Okay, how to begin? She ran her hands down the sides of her jeans as she turned to the couch, where Jamie and Kasey sat watching her anxiously. "You guys know I wasn't expecting you to come here, right? Your mom didn't have a chance to call and discuss the situation with me before she had to go away."

The boys bobbed their heads in acknowledgment of their surprise arrival. "Mama said there were some bad people looking for her and she had to go hide," one of the boys explained. "She said we would be safe here, and she would be safe where she was going."

Moistening her lips, Miranda waved a hand to indicate the small space around them. "You know how small my apartment is. One bedroom, one bath. One closet."

The boys nodded again, and one of them said, "We don't take up much room."

Miranda swallowed a sudden lump in her throat. "Oh, sweetie, I know that. You're just little boys right now, but you're growing fast. This apartment really isn't big enough for three."

"We stayed in places littler than this with Mama," the other boy asserted. "Jamie and me slept on the floor sometimes. We don't mind, do we, Jamie?"

Jamie—the one on the left, Miranda noted—shook his head vigorously. "I like sleeping on the floor."

The earnestness of his expression made her chest ache even more. "It isn't just that, Jamie. I have a job.

I have to go to my office every day. I can't stay here and take care of you."

"We can take care of ourselves," Kasey assured her. "We can make our own cereal for breakfast and our own sandwiches for lunch. We do it all the time."

Miranda sank slowly into an armchair, her gaze focused on the boys. "Are you telling me your mother left you alone when she went out?"

"Only sometimes," Kasey replied. "Sometimes we stayed with other people. But we always had food and a TV."

"And we know not to turn on the stove, and not to open the door, and not to make too much noise," Jamie said, ticking the rules off on one little hand. "And we know how to call 9-1-1."

Unable to look in Mark's direction, Miranda bit her lip. She didn't want to see Mark's reaction to the news that Lisa had been in the habit of leaving her five-year-old sons to fend for themselves, even if it was "only sometimes." She knew exactly how deeply he would disapprove—and of course, she felt the same way.

What had Lisa been thinking? Though Miranda had never imagined her sister would be nominated for mother of the year, she had assumed Lisa was at least providing basic care for the kids.

She and Lisa had agreed very early that the institution of marriage, from what they had observed, had very little to offer a modern, independent woman. They had vowed to support themselves, make their own decisions, please no one but themselves, and to remain absolutely free and unfettered at all times.

It still seemed like a good plan to Miranda—but then, she didn't have children. As far as Miranda was concerned, the plan had changed for Lisa the day her twins were born.

Lisa should have realized, and accepted, the changes that became necessary when kids entered the picture—a woman couldn't be completely free and unrestricted when she had children who were totally dependent on her. Hence, Miranda's decision to avoid them at all costs. But Lisa had chosen to keep her kids—and then continued to behave as selfishly and recklessly as she had before, leading to this situation that was a disaster for everyone involved. Not even their own dismal childhood could excuse that.

Mark, with his overly developed sense of responsibility and commitment, must be thinking terrible things about Miranda's sister. And, considering the disapproval she felt from him every time she mentioned turning the boys over to a foster home, he probably didn't think much more of *her* now.

Squirming a bit under the unblinking gazes of her nephews, she wasn't sure she thought much of herself at the moment. But then she tried to bolster her morale with the reminder that she had always been very careful not to hurt anyone with her dedication to staying free and footloose. She'd never made promises she couldn't keep, never led anyone to expect more than she was willing to give—and most importantly, she had never allowed anyone to rely on her to the extent that Lisa's children had depended on the mother who had let them down.

Miranda wasn't prepared to change that policy now.

"Look," she said, keeping her voice gentle, "I'm just going to talk to someone about finding a better place for you guys to stay, okay? Somewhere with more room, and maybe other kids to play with. I promise, I won't do anything until I'm sure you'll be well taken care of."

Both boys were shaking their heads before she even finished speaking. Tears streamed down Jamie's face. "Don't send us away, Aunt 'Randa. We want to stay with you. We'll be good. We won't make any more trouble."

"Jamie!" Miranda was honestly appalled. "You haven't been any trouble to me at all. Why would you think that?"

"Because I cried the first night and you had to sleep with us," the boy mumbled, hanging his head. "And Kasey threw up last night."

"I won't throw up anymore, Aunt 'Randa," Kasey promised. "Ever."

"We'll be really, really good," Jamie said, slipping off the couch to stand beside her chair. "We won't make noise and we'll pick up our things and we'll sleep on the floor so you can have the bed."

"We will," Kasey agreed, standing on her other side. "Just let us stay with you."

She looked helplessly at Mark. Seeming to understand that she was becoming overwhelmed, he spoke up. "Boys, your aunt loves you very much and only wants the best for you. Isn't that right, Miranda?"

She knew Mark was trying to reassure the twins. To make them understand that she wasn't sending them away through any fault of their own. Still, his words took her aback for a moment. *Did* she love her nephews? Certainly she wanted a good home for them, as she would for any innocent children, but love? She hardly knew them.

She looked from one tear-streaked little face to the other. She saw her sister's eyes. Her own dimpled chin. A deep longing for acceptance and security that she recognized all too well from her own childhood. Apparently she knew them better than she had realized. And despite that she had often told herself family ties meant nothing to her, there was still a tug of kinship when she looked at her nephews.

Love? She hadn't had a great deal of experience with the emotion. She had loved her grandmother, and she loved her sister. She couldn't honestly say she had ever allowed herself to love anyone else. Love had always seemed to be tied up with too many strings.

"Of course I want the best for you," she assured the boys, deciding to focus on the one part of Mark's statement she agreed with wholeheartedly. "And I won't agree to anything until I'm sure that's what you'll have."

She wished there was more confidence in Mark's expression when she glanced at him then. He seemed so certain she was making a mistake. His pessimism was beginning to affect her own certainty that she was making the right choice.

"Look," she said when the boys continued to sniffle and look miserable. "I haven't made any firm decisions, okay? I'm just exploring the options. So, Jamie, you and Kasey go back in and watch TV for a little longer while Mr. Wallace and I drink our coffee, okay? Don't worry about it any more right now."

As she had come to expect from them, the twins complied with her request without argument, moving into the bedroom with dragging steps and slumped shoulders, leaving her feeling like a heel.

She whirled toward Mark as soon as the bedroom door closed behind the boys. "See what you did?"

He lifted an eyebrow. "Were you not planning to tell them at all?"

"Of course I knew I had to talk to them. I was hoping to wait until later, after we'd had a nice day together."

"After they had grown even more attached to you?"

"That's not fair."

"Nothing about this situation is fair," Mark replied evenly. "Especially for them."

"You don't think I know that?" she snapped. "I'm doing my best here, Mark."

"And it's absolutely none of my business what decision you make," he said with a self-deprecating expression as he rose to his feet. "I keep saying that, and then I butt in again, don't I? I don't know why you haven't told me to get lost."

She felt herself soften. "Because I know you're genuinely concerned about the boys, of course. And because I asked for your advice."

"My advice, maybe. Not my badgering." He moved closer to her and took her hands in his. "You're going to have to do what you think best. No one else can tell you what that is. It wouldn't do you or the boys any good if you were forced into a decision that isn't right for you."

As much as she valued her independence and self-sufficiency, Miranda was oddly tempted just then to burrow into his arms and hide her face in his shoulder. Just for a little while. She was entirely confident when making decisions that affected only herself, but being responsible for two helpless children was simply terrifying.

Drawing on the reserves of strength she had depended on for so long, she squared her shoulders and looked him straight in the eyes. "Thank you for your encouragement, but you should know by now that I don't allow *anyone* to pressure me into doing anything."

He squeezed her hands briefly, then released her. "Yes, I'm well aware of that."

Rubbing her suddenly tingling palms together, she nodded toward the bar. "Your coffee is getting cold. Let me warm it up for you."

"No, that's okay. I'd better get home to my girls. And you have a game to finish," he added, motioning toward the board game still set out on the coffee table.

She wasn't sure how much fun that game would be

now, but she would do her best to keep the boys entertained and distracted for the remainder of the day.
Which wasn't going to be easy now that Mark had complicated everything, she added with another twinge of
irritation.

Call it cowardice, but she really would have pre-
ferred to break the news to her nephews at a later time.

The boys were predictably subdued throughout the
remainder of the day. Together with Miranda, they finished their game, watched an animated movie on DVD,
then had dinner—which Kasey and Jamie barely
touched. Jamie had gone very quiet again, and Kasey replied to Miranda's overtures in little more than mono-
syllables.

They were breaking her heart.

It seemed to her that every time she looked around,
she found herself gazing into two pairs of sad brown
eyes. She avoided those mournful gazes as much as
possible, busying herself with cleaning the kitchen after
dinner after sending the boys off to take their baths.
Apropos of the mood inside the apartment, rain continued to fall outside, providing a gloomy soundtrack for
the evening.

The weather had kept them in all day, but Miranda
wondered now if it would have been better to brave the
elements and go out to a movie or a museum or something. Perhaps that would have eased the trapped, restless feeling she was coping with now.

Glancing at the couch where she would spend yet another uncomfortable night, she tried to reassure herself again that she was doing the right thing. It wasn't as if she was just tossing them out for her own convenience. She would insist on talking to everyone who would be involved in placing the boys, reassuring herself that they would be well cared for. And she would follow up with them regularly, to be sure they were happy and healthy.

Maybe they could spend a weekend with her occasionally, or a holiday. Maybe Mark's lawyer client would even find a way for them to see Lisa again sometime. Surely there was something someone could do to reunite Lisa with her boys. In the meantime, they would be safe and well-tended in the foster care system.

A cold shiver ran down her spine even as that deliberately optimistic thought went through her mind.

The boys were particularly quiet when she tucked them in for the night, even though she did everything she could to cheer them up. She was tempted to make extravagant promises just to make them smile again— to assure them they would go to a house with two loving parents and happy foster siblings. That they would have a big yard to enjoy and maybe a dog like Poochie to play with.

But she refused to make promises that could prove to be false. They'd had too much of that from their mother. So, instead, she tucked them in snugly, somewhat awkwardly kissed their cheeks, and told them not to worry about anything. She would take care of everything.

She hoped they didn't hear the undertones of anxiety in her cheerful voice. Neither of them said anything in response to her babbling. They merely nestled into the covers and looked at her until she turned out the light.

She could almost feel those accusing eyes focused on her even after she closed herself into the bathroom to brush her teeth. She didn't look at the bed when she came back out, but slipped into the living room and closed the bedroom door behind her.

She couldn't concentrate on reading, so she turned on the TV, keeping the volume so low she could hardly hear it. She flipped channels until she came across a silly romantic comedy movie she had seen so many times she could quote most of the lines. She focused on that, hoping to lose herself in the story as she usually did.

It didn't work this time.

Finally giving up, she turned off the TV and the lights, stretched out as much as possible on the short couch, and pulled the quilt to her ears. The rain had stopped, so it was very quiet now, with only an occasional passing car breaking the silence outside.

After what seemed like hours, during which she tossed and turned and twisted and worried, she finally fell asleep, though her dreams were disjointed and troubling.

Something—a sound? a bad dream?—woke her sometime later. She blinked groggily, noting that the apartment was still quiet and dark except for the streetlight filtering through the blinds on the sole living room window. It wasn't raining again, so it hadn't been the weather that had roused her.

She rolled onto her side and glanced toward the bedroom door. She frowned when she saw that it stood open. She was sure she had closed it earlier.

Something made her glance down at the floor beside the couch. A dark shape blended into the shadows beside the couch. She focused intently on that figure, then sighed when she realized that one of her nephews had crept into the room with his pillow. He lay as close to the couch as he could without being underneath it, and he seemed to be asleep. He made a funny little half-snoring sound, which had probably been what had awakened her. She had no idea how long he'd been there.

She did, however, have a good guess as to his identity. It had to be Jamie.

Mark was still eating breakfast with his daughters when the telephone rang Monday morning. He crossed the kitchen to pick up the receiver. "Hello?"

"Mark?" There was an odd catch in Miranda's voice.

His pulse rate jumped in alarm. "Miranda? What's wrong?"

"I can't do it, Mark. I can't make the call. I don't…I don't…"

"Sweetheart, take a deep breath," he advised, trying to make sense of her words. "Tell me what's going on."

He heard her inhale shakily. And then she began

again, only somewhat more coherently this time. "I thought I could make the call, but I can't. Jamie slept on the floor beside the couch all night just to be closer to me. He's so scared—they both are. And, damn it, so am I. I don't know what I'm going to do with them. I don't know how we're all going to live in this little apartment or how I'm supposed to raise them when I know absolutely *nothing* about kids or…or…"

She ran out of air, and Mark took advantage of the opportunity to jump in. "I'm on my way over."

"You're busy. You have to work."

"Let me worry about that. I'm on my way."

"Thank you." The relief in her voice was unmistakable.

He disconnected, then made three quick calls. One to his housekeeper, one to his assistant and the other to his friend, the lawyer. He waited only until Mrs. McSwaim arrived, and then he kissed his girls and headed for his car.

Chapter Eight

By the time Mark arrived at Miranda's apartment half an hour later, she seemed to have collected herself somewhat. Still, she was pale when she opened her door to him, and her amber eyes were dark with emotion.

It was a measure of her distress that she reached out to him, clutching his shirt in a white-knuckled grip. "Thank you for coming. I know how busy you are, but I just really need to talk to someone."

He covered her hand with his, gripping her fingers reassuringly. "You know you can call me anytime. Where are the boys?"

"They're playing with some toys on the patio. I told them not to get off the concrete, so they can't go more than a few feet from the back door. And I can see them from the living room."

Mark had noticed the tiny patios, small rectangles of concrete attached to the back of each ground floor apartment, shaded by the same-size balconies opening off the upstairs apartments. A short lattice fence surrounded three sides of each patio, giving an illusion of privacy to those tenants who placed barbecue grills and outdoor furniture on their slabs. He was sure the twins would be fine on the patio while he and Miranda talked.

"Tell me what's going on," he said, guiding her to the couch and then taking a seat beside her. He could see through the glass doors that the boys were busily playing with a fleet of toy trucks. "I wasn't sure quite how to interpret your call this morning."

She flushed a bit, but the faintly teasing note he deliberately injected into his voice seemed to calm her even more. "Sorry. I guess I sort of lost it this morning when I realized what I had to do."

"Which is…?"

"I have to keep the boys. God help us all."

Hearing her say it made an odd warmth spread through him. He tried to ignore it as he focused intently on her taut face. "Why?"

She blinked. "Why? Because…well, they're my nephews."

"They've been your nephews for just over five years. You never had much interest in them before."

She frowned at him. "I know what you're doing. You're trying to challenge my confidence in my decision."

"Now, why would I do that?"

"To make sure I'm doing it for the right reasons, probably. You do stuff like that."

His smile felt wry. "Do I?"

"Mmm-hmm. Must be that CPA thing. Or maybe that OCD thing."

"Or maybe just the concerned friend thing," he suggested. "Why have you decided to keep them, Miranda?"

"Because I can't give them to strangers. Because I'm afraid Jamie would never recover from another abandonment. Maybe it's just because I look so much like his mother, but he has grown fond of me and it would hurt him too badly if I sent him away."

"You're underestimating your own appeal. Jamie is drawn to more than your resemblance to his mother."

She moistened her lips before continuing. "Whatever. I'm also concerned about where they would end up. I know there are some good foster homes, but what if Jamie and Kasey didn't end up in one of the better places? What if no one wanted two boys? Can you imagine how awful it would be if anyone tried to split them up?"

"That would be just short of criminal. But, for the record, I don't think they would be separated—though that might make it somewhat more difficult to place them."

Pushing her hair away from her face, she looked at him with uncertain eyes. "The thing is, when it came time for me to make that call to DHS, I just couldn't do it. I'm scared, and I'm worried that I'm not qualified to take this on—and, okay, I'm more than a little regretful at everything I'll be giving up for them. But it's the only choice I can make."

"You wouldn't be human if you didn't have regrets," he assured her, sensing that she needed more reassurance. "Remember my fantasy about escaping to a tropical beach?"

Her lips curved into just a faint suggestion of a smile. "I might have to borrow that fantasy a few times."

"Feel free." Because she still looked stressed, he reached out to take her hand in his. "For what it's worth, Miranda, I think you're doing the right thing. I know you're making a giant sacrifice, but Jamie and Kasey will always be grateful to you."

"Unless I really screw this up and ruin their lives," she muttered, leaving her hand in his.

He laced their fingers together. "You're not going to screw up. Raising kids isn't that hard. It just takes commitment, common sense, and patience. A whole boatload of patience."

The deep breath she took was a bit ragged, but it seemed to brace her. "I bet you're wishing now that you'd never asked me out Friday night," she said with a somewhat more genuine smile. "You wouldn't have ended up in the middle of all this if you hadn't been in the wrong place at the wrong time."

"Actually I'm glad I asked you out," he corrected her honestly. "Not only did I get to enjoy a very nice dinner with you that evening, but I was able to be here for you this weekend. I only hope I haven't pressured you into a decision you'll regret later."

"I'm not expecting this to be easy. And I imagine there will be times when I'll wonder if I'd truly lost my mind when I made this choice. But you didn't pressure me into the decision, Mark. I knew what you thought was the right thing to do, but I also knew you would support me if I decided I couldn't keep them."

"I would have, you know. As I told you before, you have to make the choice that's right for you and the boys."

"I think I've done that. The boys want to stay with me. I'm not sure I could live with myself if I sent them away and then found out later it was the wrong thing to do. Maybe this isn't what I would have chosen for my life at this point, but the boys didn't ask to be in this situation, either. This is where we are, and now it's up to the three of us to make the best of it."

"Sounds familiar," he said with a faint sigh, thinking of his own situation. And then he added, "You know you can count on me to help you in any way I can."

Her fingers tightened in his for a moment. "Thanks. I called this morning because I needed someone to tell me I was doing the right thing. I knew you would say I am."

"In my opinion, you are absolutely doing the right thing."

"Thanks. That helps a lot." She let her hand slip from his then, and though he regretted the loss of contact, he didn't try to hang on.

He could almost see her self-confidence returning to her, though he suspected it took quite an effort for her to square her shoulders, hold her head high and speak with a semblance of her usual confidence. "Now that I've made my decision, I know I'll be able to work everything out, so you don't have to worry that I'll be calling you every day as hysterically as I did this morning."

"I don't expect that you will."

She didn't seem to notice the slight irony in his voice. "I do need some advice to get started, if you have a little time right now."

He nodded. "I called my friend Steve, the lawyer I mentioned before, and he agreed to help you obtain legal guardianship. You'll need to take care of that before you can register the boys for day care and for school in the fall. I assume they'll be starting kindergarten then."

"Kindergarten." She said the word as if she were committing it to memory. Or perhaps adding it to a mental checklist of things she had to take care of. "When did you call him?"

"This morning, after I talked to you. I assumed from your call that you'd changed your mind about turning them over to DHS."

She nodded. "Okay. Thanks. I'll make an appointment with him as soon as I can."

"He said he would be happy to see you anytime. It doesn't have to be during office hours."

"That's very nice of him."

"As I mentioned before, he owes me a few favors. I don't mind calling one in for you and the boys."

She rubbed her temple. "I'm going to owe you plenty of favors after this. I don't know what I would have done without you this weekend. Not that I couldn't have handled it, of course," she added quickly. "But you've made everything much easier for me, and I want you to know I appreciate all you've done."

She was so determined not to sound at all dependent on him, or anyone else. Remembering what she had told him about her childhood, he could understand that. Which made it all the more special that she had felt comfortable turning to him—at least for a little while. And the fact that he was so touched worried him a bit. Miranda wasn't the only one struggling with emotions she hadn't wanted to feel.

"I'm going to have to find a place to live," she said when he remained silent. "I checked my lease, and there's a maximum of two occupants for a one-bedroom apartment. I know there aren't any two-bedroom units available now, because a friend is on the waiting list for one. My lease runs out at the end of May. I had planned to renew for another year, but I guess I'll be moving, instead."

"You're going to try to find a bigger apartment?"

"I'll pretty much have to take whatever I can find right away since I don't have much time to look around."

Mark frowned. He didn't like the thought of her being rushed into a move. What if the first place she found wasn't right for them?

"And I've got to find some sort of day care arrangement for them," she added. "I can take tomorrow off with a little rescheduling, but I have to work Wednesday. I'll have to have something arranged by then."

He was getting more concerned by the minute. It sounded as though Miranda planned to dive into this commitment headfirst. He'd hate to see her make any big mistakes at the outset of her guardianship because she didn't have the luxury of taking her time. He, as well as anyone, understood the responsibilities of work—and she certainly couldn't afford to risk her job now—but no good could come from being in too much of a rush.

Maybe he was as obsessive-compulsive as she had teasingly accused, but he thought she needed a chance to examine every option before she made any decisions.

"You and the boys can come stay with me until you find something better," he blurted, almost the moment the idea occurred to him.

Her eyes went almost comically round. "What?"

Now that he'd said it, he could see where the suggestion had merit. "You can all stay at my place for a while. I have four bedrooms. The girls can share, and the twins can take Madison's room for now. You take the final room, though I'll have to find a bed to put in it, since it's more of a playroom than a guest room at the moment. Or you can sleep in my room, and I'll take the spare."

"There's no way I'm taking your bed."

He cleared his throat—and tried to clear his mind of

several unbidden images, all of which involved Miranda and his bed. "We'll worry about the logistics later."

But Miranda was still shaking her head. "Thank you for that very generous offer, but I can't accept, of course. The boys and I aren't going to invade your household. I'll go out this afternoon and find us someplace to live."

"Think about it before you say no," he urged her. "Staying with me would give you plenty of time to find the perfect place for you and the boys to live. And Mrs. McSwaim could watch the kids while you're at work, at least until you find a better alternative. It isn't as if they're any trouble. You could pay her a little something extra, but I know she won't mind. She loves kids."

"No, really, this is too much—"

"Actually I think it's the least I can do. I consider you a friend, and friends help each other out in times of trouble. I've grown fond of your nephews. They're good kids who need a little extra attention right now. I guess I can identify with them from my own past, when I had to be separated from my mother. Some very good people helped me out then. I'd like the chance to do something like that for Jamie and Kasey."

Miranda studied his face for a long moment, and then, finally, she said, "That's a very nice offer, Mark, and I want you to know I appreciate it. I'm not sure any of my other friends would so willingly open their homes to the boys and me. But, still, I think it's better if I make other arrangements. Surely there's a decent apartment that's available by the end of the month. I'll go out this afternoon to look around."

"You have to work Wednesday. You're going to find an apartment in one afternoon, and move in the next day—while somehow arranging for day care for the boys?"

The first sign of doubt crept into her eyes, but she stubbornly shook her head. "I can handle it. And I have almost four weeks before I have to move."

"Still cutting it pretty close. Wouldn't it be better if you had time to make plans? Financial plans, as well as the logistics of where you'll live and who'll watch the boys? If you stay with me for a couple of weeks, I'll help you come up with a long-term plan. And before you get all defensive," he added impatiently, holding up one hand to forestall the speech he could see her preparing to make, "I know you're perfectly capable of doing all that on your own. I'm not trying to take over your life, Miranda, but damn it, financial planning is my job. And might I remind you that you are my client?"

"I'm sure you've helped many of your other clients make long-term financial plans—but how many of them have you invited into your home?"

"None, before now," he admitted. "But, as I've just said, I consider you a friend, as well as a client. And I know you realize this is a good alternative, but you're too stubbornly independent to accept. You seem to think you'll be under some obligation to me, or something along those lines, and that's not the case."

"I just don't like being dependent on anyone else,"

she said a bit stiffly. "And I don't like the thought of causing you so much trouble."

"I'm not going to pressure you into accepting my offer," he assured her. "I just thought it might make things easier for you if you didn't have to feel so rushed. Easier for the boys, too, if they can stay with someone familiar for the first few days after you return to work, until you have time to prepare them for whatever day care arrangements you make."

He could almost watch her mental debate playing out on her face—her reluctance to seem at all dependent on his help versus her desire to do the right thing for her nephews. He remained silent while she considered her options.

He was relieved when she sighed and nodded. "All right. For the boys' sake, I'll accept your offer, at least until I can make other arrangements. But I won't kick you out of your bed. I'll take the playroom."

"It's a deal. We can put your bedroom furniture in there for now. I'll get things ready there today, and we'll make the move tomorrow. You can leave the rest of your things here, since your rent is paid through the end of May."

The extent of his satisfaction concerned him a bit. Maybe he was getting carried away with his caretaking tendencies, especially since he knew Miranda was fully capable of making her own decisions. She was an intelligent woman who had done quite well for herself. She had put herself through college, had a good job in which she was steadily advancing, had been carefully stashing away savings for her future. The more he learned about her past and how much she'd had to accomplish on her own, the more he admired her self-sufficiency.

Was he letting his strong attraction to Miranda influence his own actions? He supposed he should be a bit more concerned about how important it had been to him for her to accept his spur-of-the-moment invitation.

But that was something else he would worry about later, he told himself as the kitchen door opened and the twins poked their heads inside.

"Aunt 'Randa?" one of them said. "We're thirsty."

She rose immediately from the couch. "Close the door and go wash your hands. I'll pour you some juice."

Spotting Mark then, the boys hurried toward him, both wearing broad smiles. He was immediately struck by the difference in their attitudes since he had left them the day before.

"Did she tell you, Mr. Wallace?" one of the boys asked eagerly. "We're going to stay with Aunt 'Randa."

"Yes, she told me."

Their obvious happiness warmed him. He hoped, for everyone's sake, that he hadn't made a big mistake in encouraging Miranda to give up the life she had so obviously loved in order to raise her young nephews.

Explaining that he had a great deal to do that day, Mark didn't stay long. Miranda spent the remainder of the morning on the phone, rearranging work schedules to give her another day off. She made lunch for the boys—peanut butter and jelly sandwiches with carrot sticks and glasses of milk, which seemed like a fairly nutritious, kid-friendly meal. They seemed to approve, since they cleaned their plates, then finished the meal with a cookie apiece.

Watching them eat with such healthy appetites, she barely touched her own food. She supposed she was still in shock that she had decided to try to raise them— not to mention that she had agreed to move in with Mark.

Okay, that didn't sound quite right, she corrected herself immediately. She wasn't exactly moving in with Mark. She and the boys were simply going to stay at his place while she looked for a more suitable apartment.

Mark had made the offer almost nonchalantly, but she knew what a big deal it really was. He was taking the risk of turning his orderly home upside down, displacing his family from their bedrooms, changing their routines, and all for a woman he had known only a year as a client.

He had told her that he considered her a friend, and that friends helped each other out in times of need. Funny. She had a lot of people she considered friends, but she hadn't even considered calling any of them for advice or assistance during the weekend. She couldn't imagine any of them so generously opening their homes to her and her two nephews.

"Can we play with Poochie when we go live with Mr. Wallace?" Jamie asked after he swallowed the last bite of his cookie. She knew it was Jamie, because she had asked them to wear different colored shirts that day. Jamie wore blue, Kasey red.

"We aren't going to live with Mr. Wallace. We're simply going to stay there for a couple of weeks until I find us a place," Miranda corrected him. "And I'm sure you can play with Poochie, but remember he's Payton's dog. You'll have to ask her permission to play with any of her things."

"Payton's kind of bossy," Kasey observed as he lowered the glass he had just drained of milk.

"Wipe your mouth," Miranda reminded him, nodding toward the paper napkin beside his plate. "And even if you think Payton is a little bossy, you two need to get along with her as best you can. It's very nice of Mr. Wallace to let us stay with him. We don't want to cause him any problems."

Both boys solemnly promised to make every effort to get along with Payton. Miranda sent them off to play while she cleaned up the kitchen, but now she was worried again about whether she had done the right thing in accepting Mark's kind invitation.

Mark worked until well after midnight Monday, trying to clear as much time as possible to help Miranda move in the next day. He didn't regret the offer he had made to her, but during the hours that had passed since she had accepted, he couldn't help thinking of all the changes that were about to take place in his household. At least temporarily.

Even though the busiest part of his work year was coming to an end, he still had quite a bit to do during the next few weeks. He would have to scramble to make up for the time he would be taking off to help her settle. And, on top of his workload for the remainder of the week, he would have three houseguests to entertain, two of them preschoolers.

As much as he loved Payton, and considered her a well-behaved child, for the most part, he knew she was going to display some territorial tendencies when her home turf was invaded. Madison didn't like change of any kind, so it would take her a few days to adapt. Mrs. McSwaim had taken the news with her usual equanimity, assuring him she could handle the extra work, but he was fully aware that he was doubling her childcare and housekeeping responsibilities—and at a time when he would be too busy to help her much.

And then there was the one consideration that *really* worried him. He would be spending quite a bit of time with Miranda Martin—in his home. And his biggest fear wasn't that he would be too badly inconvenienced during the next couple of weeks. It was that he would be reluctant to see her leave.

For the first few months he had known her, he'd tried to deny his fascination with Miranda. When that hadn't worked, he had assured himself that it was no more than a perfectly understandable physical reaction to a pretty, vibrant young woman. During the past few days, he had become painfully aware that his feelings for her were much deeper—and decidedly more dangerous—than a surface attraction.

He had a definite talent for falling for the wrong women. Last time, he had ended up with a broken marriage and two children. Now he had a responsibility to protect those children from any future mistakes on his part. So what had he been thinking inviting Miranda Martin and her nephews to move in with them, even temporarily?

Chapter Nine

"You're sure about this? You haven't changed your mind?"

Mark dragged a suitcase into Madison's bedroom— the one the twins would be using for now. It was very late Tuesday afternoon and they had already set up Miranda's bedroom furniture in the former playroom, which he had cleared out the day before. They had rented a haul-it-yourself trailer to bring the furniture over, beginning early that morning.

"For the hundredth time today," he said, "I have not changed my mind."

"I can't believe how much trouble you've gone to for us. This is well beyond the call of duty for an accountant."

He smiled a little, trying to ignore the weariness settling into his overworked back muscles. "I haven't gone to that much trouble."

Standing in the middle of Madison's bedroom, Miranda placed her hands on her hips and gave him a look of open disbelief.

Okay, so maybe he had gone to a little extra effort. While Miranda had spent yesterday packing and making arrangements for the move, he had been preparing things here for their arrival.

Both his girls had twin-bed sets in their rooms, so beds weren't an issue. He'd known Madison would be more comfortable with her own things around her, so he and Mrs. McSwaim had hauled most of her toys into Payton's room, and then had to move Payton's things around to make space.

Mrs. McSwaim had helped him prepare Madison's bedroom for the boys. They had swapped pink bedspreads for hand-pieced quilts, and replaced a few other "girly" touches with things gathered from other rooms. Fortunately the walls were painted a neutral cream color, so it hadn't been too difficult to convert the room into a welcoming temporary sanctuary for a couple of five-year-old boys.

"I didn't see this room before today, but I have a feeling it has been desissified since I accepted your invitation," Miranda remarked.

He chuckled ruefully. "I guess you could say that."

She nodded toward a collection of die-cast metal race cars grouped on a shelf that had held a row of dolls only a few hours earlier. "Yours?"

His grin deepened. "Mine. I'm a NASCAR fan. I have trouble passing up the die-cast replicas of my favorite drivers' cars. I don't know if Jamie and Kasey care anything about racing, but most boys like cars—and by the way, they're free to play with anything in here. I'm not one of those collectors who puts stuff in glass boxes and forbids anyone to touch them."

Miranda spent another minute studying the colorful array of cars, and then she said in a voice that sounded a bit strangled, "You've been so nice to us. I don't know how to—"

He dropped his hands on her shoulders and turned her to face him. "Let's just leave it at that, shall we?"

Her eyes were damp when she looked up at him. "All right. But thank you."

He couldn't resist focusing on her trembling, naturally pink mouth, and remembering that all too brief taste of her just before her nephews had arrived Friday evening. He had been hungry for more ever since.

He actually felt his head lowering toward hers when a crash of sound from outside the room made them both jump back. Moments later, Payton led the twins into the room. She was talking nonstop in the high-pitched tone she used when she was excited, and Poochie was bouncing around her feet, yipping frantically along with her. General pandemonium reigned for a few minutes, effectively putting an end to the intimate interlude between Miranda and him.

He knew he should be grateful that the interruption had prevented him from doing something that would inject awkwardness into the next few days. But he suspected that what he was feeling was much closer to disappointment than gratitude.

Mrs. McSwaim had left a chicken casserole and spinach salad for dinner. Miranda had found Mark's housekeeper to be a very pleasant woman. In her early sixties, she was short and slightly built, with an air of quiet authority that the children responded well to.

She was also a very good cook, Miranda decided, swallowing a bite of the mildly spicy casserole. No wonder Mark was so pleased with the arrangement he and his neighbor had made.

Mrs. McSwaim had insisted she didn't mind keeping the boys while Miranda worked the rest of the week. Payton would be in preschool until noon, but Mrs. McSwaim seemed to have no doubt that she could handle all four children when necessary. She seemed to find it perfectly natural that Miranda and the boys had moved in with Mark temporarily; she had even made a comment that it was nice to have friends to turn to in times of need.

That was still such a new concept for Miranda that it mystified her.

There was no need for her to make much of an effort at keeping up her end of the conversation during dinner. Payton more than fulfilled that responsibility, describing every detail of the field trip her preschool class went on that morning.

The child could certainly talk. Kasey did a pretty decent job of keeping up with her, and Jamie even said a few things when he could get a word in. Madison didn't say much, but she didn't seem as shy this time, watching with open curiosity as the others interacted around her.

Miranda turned her attention to Mark. He, too, was eating quietly, apparently paying only partial attention to Payton's chattering.

Studying his face from across the table, Miranda decided he looked tired—and no wonder. He had hauled furniture and boxes, shuffled and rearranged, while still checking in regularly with his assistant to make sure things were going smoothly in his office. Miranda suspected that his workday wasn't over yet. He had made a comment earlier about planning to do some work that evening after dinner.

Her gaze slid down his face to his mouth. He had almost kissed her earlier, before the timely interruption by the children. She had seen the intention in his eyes when he'd lowered his head toward hers…and she had held her breath, anticipating the contact. Ever since last Friday night, the thought of kissing Mark had hovered in the back of her mind. It was there still—despite her repeated warnings to herself that it was not one of her better ideas.

She supposed she should be concerned that things might get out of hand between them with her living here. But as a burst of laughter came from Payton and Kasey's side of the table, she reminded herself that they had plenty of chaperones to make sure those potentially dangerous interludes were few and far between.

Definitely for the best, she supposed. Too bad the kids' presence couldn't stop her from fantasizing about what might have been.

After dinner, Mark sent the kids into the den to watch a short animated feature on DVD while he and Miranda cleaned up the kitchen. She tried to talk him into letting her handle that on her own, but he insisted on helping out. It was something he did every evening, anyway, he told her. And, besides, he knew where everything went.

"All the munchkins seem to be starting to droop," she observed, trying to make innocuous conversation while she and Mark loaded the dishwasher. "I guess it's been a long day for everyone."

"Yeah. Payton tends to bounce off the walls when she's excited—not to mention talking a mile a minute. She wears herself out, and then she crashes."

"I noticed that she likes to talk."

Mark chuckled. "Be hard not to notice. Mrs. McSwaim thinks Payton's going to be the next Oprah."

"She could be right."

Mark measured dishwashing detergent into the dispenser and closed the doors to the dishwasher, then pressed a button to activate the wash cycle. "As soon as the video is over, it'll be time for the kids to take their baths and go to bed. That could take a while, but after they're asleep, I thought you and I could sit down and discuss some plans, if you like."

"Sure. If you have time."

"I'll make time."

She nodded briskly, trying to treat the suggestion as a business appointment. Which it was, she reminded herself. Mark had offered his services as her financial planner, and she had accepted. Looking at it that way made her much more comfortable than seeing it as a favor.

She really should ask him to bill her for his time. That would make the entire arrangement even more impersonal and keep things on a more even basis between them. If she paid for his expertise, she could feel free to ignore anything that didn't feel right for her.

She would take his advice under consideration—after all, she *had* asked for it—but she would not be told what to do.

Getting the kids bathed and tucked in took as long as Mark had warned—and then some. Payton's inevitable crash had been accompanied by whining and tears. Madison, who had been agreeable enough to the move into Payton's room when Mark had discussed it with her before, suddenly decided she wanted her own room back.

Mark had been forced to speak firmly to both his daughters before they'd settled down enough to go to bed. To repay them for the upheaval his generosity had put them through, he had read an extra bedtime story to them before tucking them in with kisses and promises that life would be back to normal soon.

He and Miranda met up again in the den. Rubbing the back of his neck, he gave her a weary smile. "Did you get the boys in bed okay?"

"Yeah, they went right to sleep. And the girls?"

"No problems," he lied airily.

"Liar. I heard Madison crying all the way down the hallway. She was upset about the twins taking over her bedroom, wasn't she?"

"Madison doesn't take well to change," he admitted. "But she'll be fine. Don't worry about it."

"I'm sorry to cause so much trouble."

"Will you stop saying that?" Hearing the slightly cross tone in his own voice, he grimaced and spoke more gently. "It isn't too much trouble. I want the girls to learn to share, and to adapt when life throws them a curve or two. This is a good experience for them."

Still not looking convinced, she nodded. "If you're too tired to talk about my plans tonight, we can—"

"I'm not too tired." He straightened his shoulders and lifted his chin in an instinctively male reaction. "Let's go into my office."

For some reason, that suggestion seemed to please her.

It was almost amusing how much more comfortable she seemed once he was settled behind his desk and she sat in the clients' chair across from him. He pulled a legal pad in front of him and picked up a pencil. "You said you wanted me to help you prepare a budget."

She leaned her elbows on his desk and propped her

chin in her hands. "Right. And you'll bill me at your usual hourly rate for doing this, of course. You should probably make a note of the time so you'll remember."

He frowned. "I'm not going to—"

"I won't let you help me unless I pay you," she interrupted flatly.

Impatience laced his sigh. "Fine," he said, making a point of looking at his watch and writing the time at the top of the page. "Now we're on the clock, so we'd better get with it."

Miranda tilted her head to eye his expression. "You look just like Payton when you pout."

"I'm not—" He made himself swallow the rest of the words.

Now that she felt more comfortable in her surroundings, she had reverted to the Miranda he had known as a client for the past year. Smart-mouthed, confident, just a bit brazen. He needed to revert to his own predinner-date persona—professional, focused, imperturbable, at least on the outside.

"Okay," he said, his pencil hovering over the paper. "What's the most you're willing to pay for rent?"

"I picked up a couple of those free apartment listings brochures yesterday. The two-bedroom apartments in the same general area where I have been living all run pretty much in the same price range." She named a couple of figures which he jotted on the pad.

"And day care?" he asked, making no comment about the rent figures. Obviously she had checked out the less expensive places; he wondered if he could talk her into letting him look them over from a safety perspective before she signed a lease. Probably not.

"Um—I don't have a clue. I haven't had time to make any calls yet."

Because day-care expenses were listed in so many of his clients' financial records, he had a ballpark idea. Miranda groaned when he gave her an estimate. "That much?"

"Good childcare is expensive, especially for two kids," he replied sympathetically. "That's why it's so difficult for many single working mothers to make ends meet."

"No kidding." She swallowed hard, then nodded. "Okay. What else?"

They spent the next half hour discussing every possible expense involved in raising two preschoolers. By that time, Miranda looked a bit pale, but grimly determined. "Anything else?"

"That should pretty much cover it—barring any unexpected expenses."

"Such as?"

"Emergency room visits, braces, glasses—that sort of thing."

"Oh. Of course." Her voice was hollow.

"Those are just possibilities, of course. With kids, you never know. You'd better see about getting them listed on your health insurance policy as soon as possible. Your premium might go up a bit."

"I'm sure it will," she said with a sigh.

"You can do this, Miranda."

"I know. It's just…a big change."

He didn't have the heart to tell her they had barely begun to discuss the changes raising twin boys would make to her life.

"I'll spend my lunch hour for the next few days checking out apartments and day-care facilities," she said, pushing a hand through her tousled hair.

"I'll ask around, see if I can come up with some recommendations for day care."

"Thank you. And now, before I forget, I want us to agree on an amount for me to pay you for our stay here, in addition to what I'm giving Mrs. McSwaim. There's the price of food and—"

He set his pencil down. "Forget it."

Her expression turned stubborn. "I insist on paying you."

"Don't tick me off, Miranda," he warned very quietly. "My home is not a hotel. I don't charge my guests to stay here."

He was well aware of what she had been doing by putting them back on an accountant-client basis. He even somewhat agreed that it was a good way to keep a careful distance between them during her stay, however brief that might be. But no way was he letting her turn him into a landlord.

Because she still looked prepared to argue, he stood abruptly, bringing the conversation to an end. "I'm sure you're exhausted after moving all day. Is there anything else I can do for you this evening? If not, I have some paperwork I need to look over before office hours in the morning."

"Oh." Looking a bit disconcerted, she stood. "I don't want to keep you from your work any longer, but I—"

He had already moved to the doorway. "What time do you usually leave for work in the morning?"

"Around seven-thirty."

He nodded. "I always have breakfast ready for the girls by seven. It's usually just cereal or oatmeal with fruit juice, but I want you to make yourself at home in the kitchen. And if you ask me for a bill for your meal, I'm liable to do something violent."

Looking resigned, Miranda shook her head. "I never realized you were so stubborn."

"Apparently you didn't know me as well as you thought you did."

"Apparently not." She studied him appraisingly for a moment, then moved toward him and the doorway. "Good night, Mark."

"If you need anything during the night, you know where to find me."

As soon as the words left his mouth, he wanted to take them back. He hadn't meant anything by them; he had simply been playing the conscientious host.

He should have known Miranda would twist his words to mean something else, entirely. Her face lit up with the wicked smile he knew so well—the one that always presaged an outrageous comment. The one that always made his own lips twitch in response.

"As tempting as that sounds," she all but purred, walking her fingertips up his chest to tickle his chin, "I think it would be best if I stay in the guest room all night."

Damn, but she could change from chilly client to sultry seductress in the blink of an eye. He had realized long before that Miranda was the only client he'd ever had who left his head spinning. She had a fairly dramatic effect on the rest of his body, as well.

It annoyed him that he couldn't switch gears as easily as she did. He was forced to clear his throat before he could say, "Good night, Miranda."

With a soft laugh, she ran a fingertip across his lower lip, then turned and walked away.

Mark sank into his chair and shoved a hand through his hair. It would probably be a good thing for his sanity if Miranda found another place to stay very soon.

Wednesday morning did not go as smoothly as Mark might have wished. Having risen early after another late night in his office, he had decided to make pancakes—his daughters' favorite breakfast when served with warmed strawberry syrup. And then he had promptly burned a batch of them, quite possibly because Miranda had wandered into the kitchen, fully dressed for work, but still looking morning-sleepy—a distracting presence.

After cleaning the griddle and successfully cooking another batch, Mark served the meal. Payton announced during breakfast that she wasn't going to preschool. She wanted to stay home and play with Madison and the twins.

"You have to go today," Mark reminded her. "Today's the final rehearsal for the end-of-the-year program tomorrow night."

"I want to stay here," Payton complained. "I already know all my lines for the program."

"But you still have an obligation to go to the rehearsal," he replied firmly. "The teachers and the other students are counting on you to be there, and you will be. You can play with Madison and the boys when you get home."

"It's not *fair!*" The words were accompanied by the kind of flounce only a four-year-old girl could pull off so expressively.

"It wouldn't be fair of you to blow off the rehearsal when everyone else is going to be there," Mark corrected her. He was aware that the boys were watching the confrontation, and that Miranda had busied herself clearing away the dishes. He really didn't want this to turn into one of Payton's rare, but formidable tantrums.

Keeping his tone firm, he said, "Come on, Payton, you know you've been looking forward to this program. You have a starring role, don't you?"

Her lower lip protruding, Payton nodded.

"I bet Kasey and Jamie would like to come see you perform tomorrow night, wouldn't you, boys?"

The twins nodded dutifully.

The prospect of a slightly larger audience brought a new spark of interest to Payton's eyes. "Will Miss Martin come, too?"

Mark wasn't so sure about that. "Oh, I—"

"Sure, Payton. I would love to come to your program," Miranda assured her. "Why not?"

"So," Mark concluded, "you have to go practice so you'll do an especially good job, okay?"

"We won't do anything fun until you get home, Payton," Jamie promised earnestly. He wore a yellow shirt today in contrast to Kasey's green.

"I wish *I* could go to preschool," Kasey murmured. "It sounds like fun."

"It is fun—sometimes," Payton conceded slowly, her temper cooling. "You've never been to preschool?"

Both boys shook their heads.

"Well, how did you learn your numbers? And your ABCs?" she demanded.

"Mama taught us our ABCs," Kasey replied. "We can write our names and count to a hundred and we know lots of songs."

"I know some of the words to 'American Pie,'" Jamie volunteered. "That's Mama's favorite song. She plays it all the time."

Mark heard Miranda gulp softly, and he had to suppress a wince at the thought of Jamie's clear little voice singing about "drinking whiskey and rye."

"You'll go to kindergarten in the fall," Miranda promised them. "You'll learn lots of new songs then."

"I'm singing some songs in the program tomorrow," Payton said quickly, making sure the topic didn't wander far from herself. "Not alone, but with my class."

She proceeded to rattle off the names of the songs they would be hearing the next evening. Relieved that the brief crisis was over, Mark told himself that he was going to have to stay vigilant in keeping Payton's tendency toward narcissism in check. She had inherited that trait from her mother, he thought with a sigh.

Mrs. McSwaim arrived soon afterward, and then it was time for Miranda to leave for work. She rather awkwardly kissed the boys goodbye and told Payton and Madison she would see them later. She left her work phone number and cell number with Mrs. McSwaim, gave Mark a cheery little wave and took off.

For the second time that morning, Mark found himself thinking of his ex-wife. Brooke had worn an expression of deep relief when she had finally "escaped" the bonds of marriage and motherhood. He suspected glumly that he had just recognized a very similar expression in Miranda's amber eyes.

Chapter Ten

It wasn't that Miranda was deliberately stalling at her office, she assured herself late Wednesday afternoon—early evening, she corrected herself with a glance at her desk clock. Almost 6:00 p.m. But she had missed two days of work, so naturally, she had a lot to do to catch up. She hadn't even had time to check out apartments during the lunch hour she had spent working at her desk.

Which didn't quite explain why she was still here, even after she had completely emptied her in-basket.

Her desk phone rang and she picked up after only a momentary hesitation. "Miranda Martin."

"Well, it really is you." Miranda recognized the voice as Brandi's. "I was wondering if you left town or something."

Miranda smiled wearily. "No, I haven't left town." She had merely left her old life behind, she thought wryly.

"We all wondered where you were when you didn't show up for Oliver's party. *Everyone* was there."

"I'm sorry I missed it." She had been too busy packing for her temporary move into Mark's house, feeding her nephews, tucking them in for the night.

"I've tried and tried to call you. I left a half-dozen messages on your answering machine. Since I don't have your cell number, I thought I would take a shot at reaching you at your office this evening. And I caught you!" Brandi added unnecessarily.

Miranda rarely gave out her cell number. She was afraid it would ring all the time if she did. "I've been busy."

"So…is there a guy?"

"Mmm." She smiled a little. "As a matter of fact, there were two guys in my bed during the weekend."

"Two?" Brandi seemed genuinely taken aback by that uncharacteristic revelation. "Um—you hooked up with two different men last weekend?"

"Actually I slept with both of them in one night. At once."

"Okay, now this is just too bizarre. If I were talking to Debbie—or even Oliver—I might believe that tale, but not you. What's really going on?"

Miranda chuckled in surrender. "Okay, I'll tell you the truth. It seems that I'm about to become the legal guardian of my five-year-old twin nephews. I've had them since last Friday night."

"You're kidding!"

"No. They're really with me. Well, not now, of course, but still in my custody."

Belatedly rethinking her initial reaction, Brandi said in a more subdued tone, "Does that mean their mother—your sister, right?—has, well, passed away?"

"No, she's—" Miranda hesitated, then said, "It's a long story, but she can't take care of them right now. There's no one else to take them, so it looks like it's up to me. I guess that means you won't be seeing me at the clubs for a while."

"Wow. This is so—" She couldn't seem to come up with an appropriate word. "What do you know about taking care of kids?"

"Nothing. *Less* than nothing. I'm completely at a loss."

"No kidding. But, er, don't ask me for help, you know? 'Cause I know even less than you do."

It was the sort of response Miranda expected from all her friends. Which only emphasized how generous Mark had been—and he was only her accountant. At least, that was the way she had tried to think of him for the past year.

"Don't worry, Brandi. I won't be asking you to baby-sit."

"Thanks. So, uh, short of that, is there anything you need?"

"No, I'm fine. But thanks for asking. Tell everyone hello for me, okay?"

"Yeah. Sure. If you ever find a baby-sitter—wow, that sounds strange—join us for an evening, okay?"

"Sure." But even as she disconnected, Miranda wondered when—or if—she would have the opportunity to hang out at a club with her pals again.

"You're sure you haven't changed your mind?"

Miranda couldn't help smiling in response to Mark's question. It reminded her of when she had asked him if he'd had second thoughts about inviting her and the boys to stay in his home. "I haven't changed my mind," she said, just as he had then. "This should be an…interesting experience."

"You've got that right," he muttered.

He unlocked the door of his SUV, which, fortunately, had a third-row seat so everyone fit inside. "Payton, be sure you have all your stuff."

"I've got it, Daddy."

Miranda looked around as she climbed out of the front passenger seat of the vehicle while Mark unbuckled and unloaded kids, swinging Madison onto his hip. The parking lot of Miss Dottie's Preschool was filling up rapidly with sedans, minivans and SUVs. Families filed toward the front door of the large, pink-sided building, preschoolers bouncing around their parents' feet and calling greetings to their classmates.

Payton joined in the chorus. "Hi, Ethan! Hi, Claire! Ms. Martin, there's my teacher, Ms. Hendricks."

With a twin clinging shyly to each of her hands, Miranda pasted on a fake smile. Apparently her brain had been working a bit slowly this week. She had just this moment realized how it would look to the other parents for her to have arrived in the same vehicle with Mark. It must appear as though Mark had brought a date to his daughter's school program.

She could almost see the speculation on the faces of people who greeted Mark when they entered the room that served as lunchroom and auditorium for the school. Folding tables had been stacked against one brightly-painted wall, and multicolored plastic chairs were lined in rows facing a small wooden stage. The chairs were filling rapidly with parents and grandparents, many holding video cameras.

The noise level was quite high as adults visited and children laughed or whined, some running around the back of the room. Taking a seat with a twin on either side, Miranda looked over Jamie's head to Mark, who held Madison in his lap. "Did you bring a video camera?"

"No." He reached into an inside pocket of the jacket he wore with an open-necked shirt and khakis. Pulling out a palm-size digital camera, he added, "I'll snap a couple of shots while Payton's on stage, but I rarely bring a video camera to this sort of thing. I prefer to experience my children's lives. I don't want to watch everything they do through a viewfinder."

Interesting philosophy—and somewhat unique these days, she mused as the preschoolers filed onto the stage and dozens of video cameras were lifted and activated.

"Aunt 'Randa," Jamie said in a loud whisper, leaning closer to her side. "I can't see Payton."

Miranda glanced at the tall woman sitting directly in front of Jamie. "Okay, let's swap seats."

They made the switch quickly, so that Miranda was sitting next to Mark with both twins on her left. Great, she thought in resignation. Now it looked even more as though she and Mark were a couple.

Deciding to leave it to him to explain to his acquaintances, she smoothed her black slacks, straightened the square neckline of her black and white color-blocked spring sweater, and then folded her hands in her lap and sat back to enjoy the program.

Well, "enjoy" might not be quite the right word, she thought a few minutes later. Listening to a bunch of four-year-olds warbling lyrics to syrupy little songs could be excruciating. Maybe her ears weren't actually bleeding, Miranda thought, suppressing a wince at one particularly high-noted passage that each performer decided to attempt in a different key and octave, but she wasn't sure her hearing would ever fully recover.

She glanced sideways at Mark. Was it possible that he actually liked what he was hearing? He was smiling toward the stage with what looked like genuine pleasure on his face. Must be a parent thing.

A reception followed the program. The children mobbed the tables holding cake, cookies, and plastic cups of pink punch, while the adults mingled and agreed that their children were all simply brilliant. With a twin clinging to each of her legs, Miranda stood to one side of Mark as several people approached him. Many of them looked curiously at her. Each time, he said simply, "This is my friend, Miranda Martin, and her nephews, Kasey and Jamie."

Miranda wondered what those other people knew about Mark's ex-wife. And whether he'd ever brought a "friend" to one of these things before—though she suspected he had not. She did not, however, have to wonder at the meaning behind the looks she got from a couple of what Miranda guessed were single moms. Undoubtedly Mark was the school's most eligible bachelor, and she noticed a few longing looks sent his way.

She couldn't blame them, really, she thought, watching as he laughed ruefully at something Payton's teacher said. The man was undeniably gorgeous. A loving father. A good provider. Just the kind of man any woman would love to find—if she happened to be looking for a partner.

She tried to talk Kasey and Jamie into mingling with Payton and her friends, but both the boys all but hid their faces in her side. It was obvious that they had very little experience with other children.

It was definitely time to get them into an environment where they would have the chance to learn to socialize. It was too late to enroll them in preschool for this year, but a day-care setting with other children their age would be good for them. And she wouldn't have to feel guilty every time she left for work, she thought with a light sigh.

By the time they had gotten the kids bathed and in bed that evening, Miranda felt as if she had just put in a sixteen-hour workday. Who would have imagined that a preschool party could be so exhausting?

She and Mark met in the hallway outside the twins' bedroom. Rubbing the back of his neck, he gave her a smile that looked tired. "I don't know about you, but I could use a drink."

"Sure, I'd love some iced tea or something."

"Actually I was thinking about something a little stronger than that."

A bit surprised, she followed him into the den. She smiled when he reached into a cabinet and pulled out the bottle of fine liquor she had given him for his birthday. Hard to believe that was only a week ago. "I thought you were going to save this for a special occasion," she commented as he poured generous measures into two tumblers.

"After sitting through that horrible program, I think we deserve it." He raised his glass in a quick salute to her, then tilted it to his lips.

Her left eyebrow rose. "You felt that way about it, too?"

"Are you kidding?" He shuddered. "Four-year-olds mangling old disco songs—man. I think I detected some sounds no human should be able to make, much less hear."

Laughing in sheer relief, she settled on the couch with her drink. "And I thought I was the only one. I don't want to be rude, but who selected those songs?"

Sitting beside her, he leaned back into the cushions and shrugged. "I just hope whoever it was gets put in charge of refreshments next year rather than music."

"Will Payton go back next year?"

"No, she'll go to kindergarten in the fall. Her fifth birthday is just before the cutoff date. But Madison will start preschool. I've already signed her up. So, I'll be attending more programs like this one in the future."

"Lucky you."

He took another sip, then chuckled. "I know you meant that facetiously, but the truth is, I do feel lucky. As awful as that program was, I still loved seeing Payton having such a good time."

"I know you did. I saw it in your face. She's a lucky little girl to have you for a father."

She had tried to speak lightly, but her words came out more wistfully than she'd intended. Must be the booze, she told herself, setting the half-empty tumbler aside. Powerful stuff.

Trust Mark to catch the emotion buried in her comment. "Didn't your father ever attend your school programs?"

She looked down at her hands. "He wouldn't have had time for frivolous things like that. My mother attended most of them—it was expected of her, after all."

Mark reached over to lay a hand over hers. "I'm sorry you had such an unhappy childhood, Miranda. And I'm sorry you're going through such a difficult time now."

She lifted her chin and spoke with the bravado she had developed through years of practice. "Hey, I survived. Just as you survived your childhood problems. The important thing is for you to make sure your girls never doubt you love them—and for me to figure out a way to make sure Kasey and Jamie don't end up in years of therapy because of my sister or me."

"You'll do a good job with them. Someday they'll understand the sacrifices you've made for them, and they'll appreciate it."

"Yes, well…" She couldn't look too far into the future. It made her too nervous, left her feeling smothered by the responsibility she had taken on. A day or two at a time, that was all she could deal with right now.

It occurred to her suddenly that his hand still rested on top of hers. And that all the children were asleep, and they were alone for the first time since their budget-planning session in his office Tuesday evening. Last night, he had retreated to his office after the kids had gone to bed, and Miranda had claimed fatigue, explaining that she was going to read for a while and then turn in early.

Maybe she should have done the same thing tonight, she thought with a thick swallow.

"I, uh, had a chance to look at a couple of apartments today," she said in an attempt to remind both of them that this was only a temporary situation.

He, too, was looking at their hands now. He moved his thumb slowly across the back of hers, making her even more acutely aware of the contact between them. "Did you find anything?"

"Not so far. Neither of the two complexes I had time to visit had anything available right now. I have a lunch meeting tomorrow, but I can probably go apartment hunting Saturday."

"Would you like some company?"

"What about the kids?"

"Mrs. McSwaim will watch them for a few hours. She likes to come over on Saturdays and do the laundry."

"She *likes* to do your laundry on Saturdays?" Miranda asked with a skeptically lifted eyebrow.

"Actually, yes. Saturdays are the most difficult days for her. She and her late husband always considered Saturday their special day. They went out for a nice lunch and then did something together every Saturday afternoon. Now, after she spends a few hours here, she and a couple of friends often go out for dinner and a movie on Saturday evenings. That keeps her busy enough that she doesn't have time to sit around and miss the old days."

"So you're actually doing her a favor by letting her do your laundry."

He laughed softly. "I'd hardly say that. I pay her well for her services—but I'm the one who ultimately benefits."

She wasn't sure why she hadn't moved her hand away yet. Why it felt so comfortable sitting side by side and sort of holding hands. She lifted her gaze to his face. Their eyes met. Held. And she became even more aware of the mistake she had made by not breaking the contact sooner.

The house was so quiet. As if they were the only ones in it. The couch had seemed larger when they'd first sat down; now she realized that they were actually sitting quite close together.

Twice they had almost kissed. Both times they had been interrupted. Here was their chance to try again…if they were reckless enough to do so.

She had always known she had a reckless streak.

"I know the program tonight wasn't your sort of thing," Mark said without looking away from her. "But it was nice of you to go. Payton loved having more people to show off for."

"It wasn't so bad. I thought the kids were cute— though it would have been nice to have a 'mute' button. I suppose I'll have to go to things like that for the boys, so it was good practice."

"It will mean a great deal to them to have you there for their activities. They won't have to think back, the way you do, and remember times when no one was there to cheer them on."

"You're making me sound noble again. That worries me."

"Why?"

"I'm still afraid I'll mess up," she admitted.

"You'll make plenty of mistakes. Do things you'll regret. Say things you'll wish you could take back."

"Oh, *that* makes me feel better."

"Sweetheart, we all make those kinds of mistakes. Anyone with kids can tell you that guilt and worry and uncertainty are all part of the package."

He was making her think about the future again. And once again, she was starting to feel suffocated.

One day at a time, she reminded herself.

"Anyway…" she began. His eyes were such a pretty

gray. She lost herself in them for a moment, and promptly forgot what she had intended to say.

"Anyway...?" His thumb moved slowly across her hand, leaving little ripples of electricity across her skin.

She moistened her lips. "Um...Mark?"

He was looking at her mouth now. "Yeah?"

"We should probably go to bed."

That brought his eyes to hers again. "You can't imagine how often I've fantasized about you saying that."

And she had thought *she* had the reckless streak. She was both startled and annoyed to feel her cheeks warm. How long had it been since anyone had actually made her blush? Junior high?

She frowned at him. "You warned me once that you were going to call my bluff someday just to see what I would do. Maybe I'd better give you that same warning, since you seem to be getting a bit overconfident lately."

"Are you calling my bluff?" He seemed intrigued by the idea.

She should. She really should. Just to watch him squirm, since she doubted he was any braver than she was about actually taking their foolhardy flirtations to the next level.

He smiled when she remained silent. It was a smile that held both wry amusement at their foolishness, and a touch of regret that no bluffs would be called this evening—or at any time in the foreseeable future.

He looked down at their hands again, and she followed his glance automatically. His fingers looked so long and strong over hers. Clever fingers when they danced over a keyboard or a calculator. Just the thought of having those long, clever fingers dancing over her skin was enough to make her breath catch.

She really should move her hand. And she would. In just a moment.

"I knew it wouldn't be easy being in the same house with you," he murmured.

"It was your idea," she reminded him in little more than a whisper.

"I know. I figured I was strong enough to resist temptation."

"And are you?"

"I hope so. But first, there's something I just have to get out of my system." He leaned forward, tilted her chin upward, and covered her mouth with his.

She had seen the kiss coming. She could have stopped him had she really wanted to. She had no doubt that he would back off immediately if she gave him the slightest signal to do so. But she didn't.

Maybe this was something she needed to get out of her system, too.

The kiss had been building for quite awhile—probably even before their date. Attraction had been strong between them since the first time she had walked into his office. She had flirted outrageously with him that day, enjoying his disconcerted reactions. Even then she had figured nothing would come of it; the photographs on the credenza behind his desk had given her a clue that this was not a man who fit her "safe date" profile.

How could she have known how circumstances would intervene so that she'd end up actually living in the same house with him? Not exactly dependent on him—she wouldn't accept that—but certainly grateful for his assistance.

It seemed that fate had called both their bluffs.

It didn't surprise her in the least that Mark was one heck of a kisser. Not too hard, not too soft. Not too aggressive, but assertive enough to excite her. He waited until she parted her lips for him before he deepened the kiss—and then he took full advantage of the invitation.

He even knew exactly what to do with his hands. Not too grabby, like Robbie, on the one date she'd had with the guy. But he didn't just let them lie there, either. Mark's hands slid slowly up and down her back, from her shoulders to the curve of her hips. A pleasurable, unhurried massage that made her whole body ache for more.

She certainly hoped Mark was strong enough to resist temptation, she thought as she wrapped her arms around his neck and tilted her head to take the kiss to another level. She wasn't at all sure that she was.

Oddly enough, it was a completely errant thought that pulled her out of the moment. Something to do with the conversation she and Mark had just had about Mrs. McSwaim. The woman who would rather spend her Saturdays doing another family's laundry than sitting alone with the memories of the man she had loved and lost.

Her eyes opened. A moment later, she sat several

inches away from him, so that she was all but pressed against the arm of the couch.

"Well…" She cleared her throat. "Now that we've gotten that out of the way…"

It probably shouldn't have pleased her so much that it took him a moment to collect himself enough to answer. His voice was still husky when he asked, "Something I did…?"

"No. Something you said. Sort of." She jumped to her feet, and mentally blamed the slight unsteadiness of her movements on the liquor. "I'm going to bed. I'll see you tomorrow."

"Miranda?"

"Good night, Mark." She didn't look back on her way out of the room, though she knew he watched her until she was out of sight.

Chapter Eleven

Though she didn't have time to look at apartments Friday, Miranda had a chance that afternoon to call a few of the day care facilities from the list Mark had prepared for her. She was dismayed, but not terribly surprised, to learn that several were already booked to capacity for the summer. One she crossed off the list just because she didn't like the patronizing tone of the woman she spoke to.

After just over an hour, she had appointments to visit two places Monday afternoon. Both were more expensive than she had hoped to find, but they offered enhanced programs, rather than just baby-sitting. The boys would have the chance to participate in arts and crafts, ice-skating, gymnastics, and swimming lessons, and museum and children's theater visits. Those opportunities seemed worth the extra expense.

After all, Miranda thought with a sigh as she pushed the telephone aside and turned back to her computer, she wouldn't be spending much on her personal entertainment for a while. Might as well spend it on the boys.

As tempted as she was to dawdle at the office to avoid any more awkward encounters with Mark, she couldn't be that heedless of her responsibilities. She left at her usual time, telling herself she would make certain Mark couldn't tell that their kiss had haunted her ever since she had all but bolted from the den last night. An extra dollop of makeup had camouflaged the results of a restless night, and she had managed to get through a hasty breakfast without making a complete fool of herself. Barely.

She would have to make sure they didn't end up alone again this evening. Because when it came to Mark Wallace, her willpower was most definitely precarious.

Miranda insisted on clearing the dinner dishes Friday evening, telling Mark she didn't need any help this time. For once, he didn't try to argue with her. All in all, it seemed wiser to keep a safe distance between them, using the children as buffers whenever possible.

It was a nice, warm evening, the sun still bright at just before seven. While Miranda worked in the kitchen, Mark took all four kids into the backyard to play.

The family from whom he had bought the house

had poured a concrete slab in one corner of the large, fenced yard to serve as a mini basketball court. They had left a metal pole behind, and Mark had installed a net at regulation height for the occasional game with visiting friends. A child-height net was set up at the other end of the concrete.

While Madison toddled around the yard pushing a plastic toy lawnmower, Mark watched as Payton and the boys threw basketballs at the shorter goal. His eyebrows lifted when he noticed that the boys rarely missed.

"You two are pretty good," he said to the nearest twin.

"We like to shoot hoops," the boy replied. "Can we shoot at the big goal?"

"Which one are you?" He hated having to ask, but he'd forgotten which twin wore a white T-shirt today and which wore blue. Now that Jamie had gained more confidence, the boys were almost impossible to distinguish by behavior.

"I'm Kasey. Do you want to play with us on the big goal?"

Curious about whether the boys could shoot that high, Mark nodded. "Sure. Why not?"

"We can play 'Donkey.' We played that all the time with Mama."

"'Donkey?' I've never heard of that game."

"Like 'Horse,' only you spell Donkey. D-o-n-k-e-y," Kasey explained earnestly—just in case Mark didn't know how to spell the word, apparently. "Every time you miss the basket, you get a letter, and the first one to get a Y is the donkey and he loses."

Mark grinned. "Okay. That sounds easy enough."

Kasey pointed a warning finger at him. "Don't let us win. Mama never let us win, and we beat her all the time."

"Don't worry. I always play to win."

Jamie giggled. "You sound just like Aunt 'Randa."

"Yeah, well...um, who's going first?"

"I don't wanna play," Payton announced disgruntledly. "I can't hit the big basket."

"Then you can play with Poochie and Madison for a few minutes," Mark instructed.

"Jamie can go first," Kasey offered. "I'll go second. And Mr. Wallace, you go last, 'cause you're the oldest. And we get to stand a little closer than you do, because we're shorter."

Nodding, Mark reflected that Kasey made a habit of looking out for his brother. He wondered if Kasey had been born first.

Jamie took the ball, bounced it a couple of times, then stood at the closer line with an amusingly intense look of calculation on his face. A moment later, the ball sailed through the air and fell through the hoop.

Jamie whooped and pumped a fist. "All right! Nothing but net."

"Not bad," Mark acknowledged.

Kasey took his place at the line, frowned exactly the way his brother had, and threw the ball. Mark found himself holding his breath when the ball circled the rim a few times, and then dropped through. Kasey did a little victory dance, high-fived his twin, then grinned at Mark. "Let's see you beat that, Mr. Wallace."

"Why don't you just call me Mark," he suggested, taking the ball. "There's no need to be so formal when I'm about to show you losers who rules this b-ball court."

Both boys grinned and hooted in derision at the challenge, and Mark could tell they were enjoying the male attention. He really was becoming quite fond of these quirky twins—which didn't mean he was going to let them turn him into a "Donkey," he thought as he took his place at the regulation free-throw line and shot the ball cleanly through the hoop.

Miranda watched the game through the kitchen window. Even from there, she could tell the boys were having a great time bonding with Mark. She watched as Mark picked one of them up and dangled him, laughing and squirming, upside down.

Though she enjoyed seeing her nephews beaming with joy, she couldn't help wondering again what their lives would be like after she moved into a new place. They would be in day care between eight and ten hours most days—and no matter how "enhanced" the programs, it wasn't the same as being at home. They would be living in an apartment building, not a big house with a fenced yard for safe outdoor play. And she would be the responsible adult in their lives—the scariest prospect of all, in her opinion.

Though she worried about the twins, it was Mark her gaze lingered on as she watched the horseplay outside. He seemed to be having a great time playing with the boys. His hair was breeze-tossed, making it curl more than usual around his face. She liked those curls, though she suspected he made a deliberate effort to tame them every morning. But then, she liked everything about him, she thought, watching the muscles ripple beneath his gray T-shirt as he demonstrated a lay-up shot for the twins.

She was beginning to worry more all the time about the extent of her growing feelings for him.

It had always been so easy for her to walk away from any relationship that had become potentially complicated. But Mark Wallace was different from the men she had dated so casually before—something she had known from the first time she'd met him. Which was exactly the reason she had been so resistant to getting involved with him. And why she was still so determined to keep her feelings for him under control.

Observing him chase the boys around the yard in a laughing game of keep-away with the basketball, she knew she had better move out soon, before things got out of hand between them.

She wanted to go out and play with them. Because she could so easily picture herself out there laughing with Mark and the children, she made herself turn away from the window.

This wasn't where she belonged, she reminded herself. It wouldn't be fair to any of them to pretend otherwise.

* * *

They had just gotten all four kids bathed and sent off to bed when the doorbell rang at just after nine.

"That will be Steve," Mark said, meeting Miranda in the hallway outside the twins' bedroom. "I'll let him in. We'll be in the kitchen when you're ready to join us."

Though Miranda had known his friend would be stopping by this evening, she seemed a bit surprised by his choice of venue for the meeting. "The kitchen?"

He smiled and nodded. "Steve always arrives hungry. I'll serve him coffee and some of that pecan pie Mrs. McSwaim made today."

"Okay. I'll be right down." She moved toward her bedroom.

"Don't forget the letter from your sister. He'll need to see that."

Miranda nodded and disappeared into the bedroom, while Mark hurried down to usher his attorney friend, Steve Petty, into the house.

"Nice of you to come, Steve."

His tall, almost painfully thin attorney friend shrugged, his smile lighting his typically somber, dark-chocolate-hued face. "You know I still owe you plenty of favors after what you did for my parents last year."

"Would you quit that? You paid me for straightening out their books."

"I still think you undercharged us. Dad had those books in such a mess that they'd have lost everything if you hadn't helped them."

"They're doing okay now?"

"Dad's doing as well as can be expected. Selling the store took a lot of pressure off. He was able to hide his condition for a long time, because he made all the decisions for the store without consulting anyone. But at least we were able to step in before he had to declare bankruptcy. They made a little profit on the sale, and they got to keep their house, so it all worked out all right."

There was sadness in Steve's voice, which Mark knew was due to his father's gradual slide into the mental ravages of Alzheimer's, but there was also relief that total financial disaster had been averted.

Sensing a change of subject was in order, Mark asked, "How does a serving of Mrs. McSwaim's homemade pecan pie sound?"

"Like a little slice of heaven," Steve replied promptly. "Especially if you've got some vanilla ice cream to go on top of it."

"It just so happens you're in luck. And I made a fresh pot of coffee to go with it. Decaf, since it's so late. Miranda's going to join us in the kitchen."

"So," Steve said, taking a seat at the kitchen table while Mark pulled dessert plates out of a cabinet. "Tell me about this friend of yours. Is she pretty?"

"You can judge that for yourself."

"I'd rather know what you think."

Mark closed the freezer door. "Yes, she's pretty."

"Oh?"

"And she's a friend. Nothing more," he added, anticipating the next question.

"Your idea, or hers?"

"Just eat your pie." Mark thumped the plate holding a generous serving of pie à la mode in front of his friend and turned to fill a cup of coffee to go with it.

Steve had just swallowed the first bite, murmuring his appreciation, when Miranda came in carrying a bulging manila envelope. A gentleman to the toes of his polished shoes, thanks to a mother who had drilled old-fashioned Southern manners into him, Steve rose to his feet.

"Don't get up." Miranda gave him one of her golden-bright smiles and motioned for him to sit back down. "You must be Mark's friend, Steve Petty. I'm Miranda Martin."

Steve sent Mark a look that wasn't hard to interpret. Steve was obviously thinking that Mark had been holding out when he had described Miranda as merely "pretty." "It's very nice to meet you, Ms. Martin."

"Please call me Miranda."

"As long as you'll call me Steve."

Wryly aware that his friend was rapidly succumbing to Miranda's charm, Mark placed a slice of pie and a cup of coffee in front of Miranda without bothering to ask if she wanted any. He already knew she had a sweet tooth, despite her willowy figure.

He would have left them alone but she had asked him to sit in when he'd told her that Steve had agreed to stop by tonight. She wanted him to ask any questions she might overlook, she had explained.

But it turned out that Mark had very little to contribute during the meeting. Miranda was well prepared, providing all the documentation Steve requested and asking plenty of questions on her own. By the time the consultation ended, Miranda and Steve were getting along like old pals, and Mark was feeling more than a little superfluous.

Miranda really was quite capable of handling her own affairs. He knew she appreciated what he'd done for her, but she would have gotten by just fine on her own, one way or another. Despite her occasional attack of nerves, she knew it, too.

He saw her gaining confidence with the boys with every passing day. No surprise, since they were so easy to care for, at least at this stage. Tomorrow she would probably find an apartment, and after that, she would be on her own again. He supposed he should be pleased for her.

He wished he could say he was.

"I like your friend," she told him after Steve left.

"He's one of the good guys," Mark agreed. "He handled my divorce a couple of years ago, but I've known him even longer. About five years now, I guess."

"Is he married?"

"No. He's involved in a serious relationship, though. I wouldn't be surprised if they announce an engagement soon. Er…why do you ask?"

"Just curious. Well…good night, Mark."

"You're turning in so early? It's barely ten."

"I think I'll read awhile before I turn in. Maybe watch the news to see what the weather's going to be like tomorrow. I'll see you in the morning."

"All right. Good night." He watched somewhat wistfully as she turned and headed up the stairs.

He knew what she was doing. Trying to avoid being alone with him again. Wise move, of course—which didn't mean he had to like it.

He knew there was a chance they'd have ended up kissing again had she stayed. He knew he looked at Miranda with the same hunger Steve had displayed for Mrs. McSwaim's pecan pie. And he knew that what he wanted from Miranda involved a lot more than a few kisses.

Following that line of thought was dangerous. He knew it—but he spent plenty of time doing it, anyway.

He reminded himself that his girls' interests came first. Letting them get too accustomed to having Miranda and the boys around, would be totally irresponsible of him. Payton and Madison had already loved and lost one woman who saw them as unwanted encumbrances. He wouldn't let that happen again.

Now if only he could believe that it was not too late to prevent *himself* from falling completely under Miranda's spell.

Saturday morning did not have an auspicious beginning. Madison woke up cranky. She whined all the way through breakfast, clinging to her father and fussing whenever he tried to set her down.

Mark offered to stay home to entertain her, but Mrs. McSwaim insisted that he accompany Miranda on the apartment-hunting excursion.

"I can take care of Maddie," she assured him. "You go help Ms. Martin. You know how those people take advantage of a young woman on her own. They won't try to pull anything if she has you there to back her up."

Miranda was not at all pleased by the implication that she needed a man to make sure she didn't fall for a hard sell. She reminded herself that Mrs. McSwaim was of another generation, when women had been trained to think of men as their protectors.

The older woman persuaded Mark to go with Miranda, even though she tried to convince him that she was perfectly capable of going alone.

"I'm sure you have no need of my help at all," he replied somewhat wryly. "But I would still like to come with you, if you don't mind having me tag along."

It would have seemed rude to turn him down, especially when Mrs. McSwaim was standing there beaming with such satisfaction. Miranda managed a strained smile and assured him that she would be glad for the company.

"I want to go! I want to go!" Payton jumped up and down in entreaty.

"Not this time," her father replied. "I'll take you somewhere later."

Payton sulked. "But I want to go now."

"Don't give me trouble over this," Mark warned her. "Stay here and help Mrs. McSwaim with Madison. No arguing."

Payton looked as though she would have liked to risk a debate, anyway, but something in her father's voice must have let her know he wasn't in the mood to tolerate a tantrum. Her lip remained firmly in pout position, but she kept quiet.

Kasey tugged at the hem of Miranda's shirt. "Can we go? We want to see where we're going to live."

She could understand his point, but she suspected that letting the twins go when Payton had been turned down would cause a scene. "You'd better stay here this time. Mark and I will scout out some places, and if I find one, I'll take you to see it, okay?"

For just a moment, Miranda thought Kasey was going to argue, which would have surprised her. Jamie gave his twin a frown, and Kasey subsided into a pout that rather resembled Payton's.

Maybe they'd had a bit too much of each other lately, she thought.

After two hours of driving from one apartment complex to another, Miranda thought she'd had a bit too much of Mark. He found something wrong with every place they visited. This one was on a street with too much traffic. That one had no good place for the boys to play. Another had a drainage problem in the parking lot.

Miranda sighed in frustration when they left the fourth complex—which he said was too small for a family of three. "I can't afford a fancy town house, Mark. I'm going to have to settle on someplace eventually."

"There are dozens of apartment complexes in the

Little Rock area," he replied without concern. "You'll find the right place if you're patient and discriminating."

"You are aware that, while I'll certainly take your advice under consideration, the final decision of where I'm going to live is mine?"

"Of course. I'm just trying to make myself useful by pointing out problems you might overlook if you're in too much of a hurry."

Glancing away from the road ahead for a moment, she gave him a sideways glance. His expression looked innocent enough, but she still wasn't convinced he wanted to help her find an apartment today. It seemed to her that he would have been anxious for her to move out of his house, so he could get his life back to normal again. But that wasn't the way he was acting.

He watched as she turned right at a busy intersection. "Where are you going now?"

"I need to stop by my apartment for a minute while we're here in the neighborhood. I left some files there that I need for Monday. It will just take me a few minutes to check the mail and my phone messages and get what I need."

"Take as long as you want. It didn't take much time to check out the apartments we've seen so far today."

Thanks to him hurrying her through them as if she'd had a deadline to meet, Miranda thought. "Maybe we'll have time to look at a couple more places on my list today."

"Sure, why not?" He sounded agreeable, if not exactly eager.

Reminding herself that he was the one who had been so determined to accompany her on this outing, she parked in front of her old apartment and turned off the engine. Before she could ask if he wanted to come inside with her, he had his seat belt off and the car door open.

Chapter Twelve

Miranda checked her mail on the way to her apartment, pulling out the bills and catalogs that had accumulated since she'd stopped by two days earlier. With Mark right behind her, she unlocked the door of her apartment—hers for another few weeks, anyway—and stepped inside.

The apartment already had the slightly musty smell of vacancy, she noted with a tinge of sadness. She had enjoyed living here. Too bad there wasn't a suitable apartment in the same complex for her and the boys.

Motioning for Mark to have a seat on the sofa, she punched the play button on her answering machine. Apparently word had gotten out—thanks to Brandi— that Miranda's social life would be severely curtailed for the foreseeable future. There were only a couple of messages, both inviting her to parties, both from people who didn't know Brandi. Normally the recorder would have been nearly full after two days, Miranda reflected with another wave of nostalgia for her old, carefree life.

The files she needed were in her closet. She paused in the bedroom doorway, struck by the emptiness of the room now that the bed and dresser had been moved out. She was moving away from the life she had built for herself a little piece at a time, she thought wistfully. It wouldn't be long before someone else's things filled these rooms.

She told herself it was silly to be so attached to this tiny apartment. She'd only lived here a couple of years, and she'd spent more time out with her friends than in these rooms. But it had been home to her, more so than the house in which she had grown up with her family. She would miss it.

She hadn't realized Mark had moved close behind her until he laid his hands on her shoulders. "A few regrets?"

"I guess so."

"That's only natural."

"So you keep telling me."

His hands moved on her shoulders, kneading the knots that had formed there. "You must feel as though a tornado has swept through your life and changed everything."

The massage felt good enough to make her almost purr her answer. "That pretty well sums it up."

His thumbs rotated at her nape, eliciting a murmur of pleasure. "What you need is a break from worrying about everything. Why don't you take tonight off and go to one of those parties? I can watch the kids for a few hours."

A sound of sheer exasperation escaped her. "Damn it, Mark, stop that."

His hands froze. "The massage?"

"No. Yes." Stepping away from his touch, she turned to face him. "Stop doing so many nice things for me. You've already taken my nephews and me into your home. You've moved furniture, rearranged your schedules, cooked for us...and now you're offering to baby-sit so I can take a break and go to a party."

"And this annoys you...why?"

"Because I'm not sure why you're doing all this. I know you have a habit of doing nice things for people— but would you have done this much for any other client? Or do you think I need your help more than most, that I can't take care of things on my own?"

"I have no doubt that you would be fine on your own. I just wanted to help, if I could. Because—well..."

"Because?" she prodded, eyeing him suspiciously.

He sighed. "Oh, hell. It's easier to show you than to tell you."

While she was still trying to figure out what he meant, he reached for her.

She should have known that the emotions that had been building between them would explode eventually. She *had* known, actually—which was why she had tried not to be alone with him since the last time they had almost given in to temptation.

She had thought an apartment-hunting excursion would be safe enough. She should have known better, she thought as he crushed his mouth against hers.

She could still end this before it went too far. One move on her part to stop him would be all it would take to have him backing away. But when he lifted his head to take a quick breath, she was the one who reached up to take his face between her hands and pull his mouth back to hers.

The kiss became more heated, more intense. Miranda's pulse raced as she drew closer to him, wanting to feel him against her. His hands moved over her in a more sensual massage than the brief neck rub that had felt so good before. She had purred with pleasure then, but she was very close to moaning now.

She loved the feel of his thick, slightly curly hair. There had been plenty of times during the past year when she had been tempted to plunge her hands into it—and it felt every bit as good as she had imagined it would.

He shifted so that her back was pressed against the bedroom wall, and then he leaned into her. It never failed to surprise her that her "buttoned-down accountant" had such a hard, strong body beneath his conservative clothing.

Speaking of which…she felt his right hand slip beneath the hem of her short yellow T-shirt. His palm was warm against her waist, and when he slid his hand upward, she arched forward into his touch. He slid his knee between her legs. Even through layers of denim, the contact made her ache for more.

He tore his mouth from hers and buried it in her throat, his lips moving against her skin when he said, "We really should stop this now."

She slid her hands down his back, her fingertips sliding over the ridges of bone and muscle. Her eyes were closed, enhancing the tactile sensations. "Not yet."

A tiny nip at her collarbone made her shiver. "Miranda." There was a raw edge to his voice now. "You're treading on thin ice here. It's been a while for me…"

She rubbed her cheek against his springy hair. "For me, too."

For some reason, no man had intrigued her enough for her to risk a potentially sticky intimate involvement. It had been…well, more than a year now, she realized with some surprise. Since she had met Mark Wallace, actually.

"So…" He nibbled kisses down the line of her jaw, his fingertips brushing the fabric of her bra.

She all but melted into a puddle at his feet as her nipples drew into hard, aching points. "So…" she whispered, and pulled his mouth back to hers.

She could not have said later who first reached for buttons and snaps and zippers. Or whose clothing fell aside more quickly beneath the onslaught of eager, impatient hands.

The absence of a bed didn't discourage them; they tumbled to the plush carpet, rolling fluidly across it. Between kisses and gasps, Mark muttered something about protection. Tangling her legs with his, she informed him that she was on the pill. When it came to pregnancy, she took no chances, even when she hadn't been involved with anyone in more than a year.

Considering how long they had waited, it was no surprise that their lovemaking was fast and rather frantic. Both of them were primed for release, and they achieved satisfaction almost simultaneously, their mingled cries echoing in the nearly empty room.

Sprawled beneath Mark's damp body, Miranda wondered dazedly if she would be able to walk again within the next few hours. There was a distinct possibility that she was going to have to stay right where she was for a while.

Feeling Mark's warm rapid breath still against her cheek, she decided she had no complaints.

After a long moment, he sighed heavily and rolled onto his back. "Oh, man."

She smiled faintly. "Thank you. I think."

Gazing meditatively at the ceiling, he said, "I can't feel my legs."

She laughed softly. "Give me a minute and I'll feel them for you."

"Damn, woman, are you *trying* to kill me?"

Giggling, she rolled onto her side to kiss his cheek. "We don't have time for any more 'feeling around' right now, anyway. Especially not if we're going to see a couple of more apartments before we go relieve Mrs. McSwaim."

"Oh." His voice was suddenly hollow. "Yeah, I guess you're right."

Determined to play this scene lightly, Miranda reached for her clothes. "I won't take long in the bathroom. Then you can have it while I gather the things I need to take with me."

He caught her wrist when she started to rise. "Miranda…"

"Mmm?"

Searching her face, he asked uncertainly, "Just what was this for you?"

Hesitating for only a moment, she said, "It was a very nice distraction. Thank you."

His hand fell heavily from her arm. There was little expression in his voice when he replied, "You're welcome."

She escaped to the bathroom with her clothing bundled in her arms.

She deliberately kept her mind blank while she quickly cleaned up and dressed. Allowing herself to dwell only on the relaxed and mellow way she felt, she assured herself that nothing had really changed between Mark and her. They had scratched an itch that had been bothering both of them, that was all.

But because that sounded so wrong even to her, she cleared her mind of any thought except the other apartments she hoped to tour that day. She really needed to find another place to live very soon—before her life became even more entangled with Mark's.

* * *

There was only time for one other apartment visit before they returned to Mark's house. For the first time all day, Mark could find very few flaws to point out— or maybe he was simply too distracted to look closely this time.

He couldn't take his brooding gaze off of Miranda.

How could she be so blasé about what had happened between them today? She seemed to be totally focused on checking out the size of bedrooms, bathrooms and closets, exploring the kitchen and pantry, approving the pool, exercise room and playground facilities. She seemed pleased to learn that a ground-floor two-bedroom apartment would be available next week.

"I think this is it," she told Mark with a smile that appeared completely genuine. Buddy to buddy. "I can totally see me living here with the boys."

And did she see him fitting anywhere into that picture? As a good friend? An occasional visitor? Or just her accountant again? For all he knew, she might even end the business relationship now that they had stepped over a line she had never intended to cross.

A very nice distraction. Was that really all it had meant to her?

Unfortunately it had meant a great deal more to him.

He tagged along behind Miranda and the apartment manager on a tour of the property, basically ignored by both of them. Miranda had made it clear this time that he was just a friend along for the outing, and that her opinion was the only one that counted, so the manager concentrated on selling the complex's assets to Miranda.

"I'm sold," Miranda said when they returned to the leasing office. "I think my nephews and I will be very comfortable here."

She looked at Mark as if daring him to argue, but he merely nodded. "It does seem like a nice place."

It almost seemed to surprise her that he hadn't found any faults, but after a moment she smiled and turned back to the manager. "What do I need to do to reserve the apartment?"

So she had made up her mind. She wanted to move out of his house in a few days. Everything would be back to normal in his life. Comfortable. Predictable. Lonely.

"I'll call a moving company to transfer the rest of my things to the new apartment," Miranda mused aloud when they were back in the car. "I know there isn't all that much, but it will be easier just to have someone come in and do it all at once. And I'll need to buy furniture for the boys' bedroom, and call the electric company and the telephone company—and the cable TV people. And I'll need to change my address for my insurance and my subscriptions and other bills. What else?"

She seemed to be babbling to fill the silence, but he went along. "You can make a list, adding to it as new thoughts occur to you. It will take a few weeks to get everything settled, but it will all work out."

"I'm sure you're right. I have two day-care appointments Monday, so maybe I'll have that resolved by then. Both places are open from 7:00 a.m. until 7:00 p.m. during the summer. I'll make sure my office hours correspond."

"And when you have to leave town?"

"I've been thinking about that, too. My clerical assistant is a single mom with a seven-year-old son. Money's tight for her, so I think she would be willing to watch the twins occasionally for a little extra income."

"She's trustworthy?"

Miranda shot him a look. "I wouldn't even consider asking her if I didn't think so. Give me some credit, Mark."

"Sorry. I didn't mean to imply that you would be careless about their safety."

"Good." She looked back at the road ahead, her fingers tight around the steering wheel.

"You know the boys are always welcome at my house. I hope you'll feel free to call if you ever need someone to watch them."

"Thanks, but I think I've got everything under control."

"You always do," he muttered, unable to mask his growing annoyance with her.

She glanced at him again, but didn't seem to have anything to say.

"About what happened between us earlier…" This was hardly the best time to bring it up, but they would be back at his place in a few minutes, surrounded by kids. And he suspected that Miranda would make sure they weren't alone together again.

"It really was very nice, wasn't it?" Her tone was so cheerful and airy, they could have been talking about the weather. "Of course we can't let it happen again, but I guess we both needed to cut loose for a little while."

Cut loose. That ranked right up there with a "nice distraction," in his opinion. Either way, it denoted a complete lack of commitment. An absence of emotion. He didn't know whether she actually felt that way, or was simply afraid to admit there was more to it. He was worried he would drive her even further away if he admitted that their lovemaking had meant a great deal more to him than it apparently had to her.

"Miranda—"

He watched as her fingers flexed on the wheel, her knuckles going white. "I can't do this now, Mark," she cut in before he could say anything more. "There's too much change going on in my life. Too much turmoil. I can't deal with all of that and you, too."

His first instinct was to be offended by those blurted words. But after mentally replaying them a couple of times, he realized that she had just implicitly admitted that making love with him had *not* been a casual thing. He should have realized sooner that her chatty, almost hyper behavior ever since they'd left her apartment had been a clue to how shaken she was.

She wasn't pushing him away because it had been a casual encounter for her—but because it had not been casual at all. He supposed that should make him feel better, but either way she was pushing him away.

He would have liked to argue his case further. To make her admit that she cared—if only a little. And to try to convince her to give them the opportunity to see where these feelings took them. But because he had heard the slight note of desperation in her voice when she had told him she couldn't handle any more changes in her life now, he bit back the words.

For Miranda's sake, he would put his own desires aside for now. She needed him to be a friend—so he would be a friend. That was just the kind of guy he was, he told himself with uncharacteristic bitterness.

It was just after two o'clock when Miranda and Mark returned to his house Saturday afternoon. Still very early in the day, Miranda mused with a glance at her watch as they entered the house. Amazing how many things had changed in such a few hours.

But she couldn't think about that now, she told herself. She planned to spend the rest of the day working very hard to avoid thinking about it.

Things had not gone smoothly while they were out. Madison's morning crankiness had developed into a runny nose, a scratchy throat and a fever. Looking flushed and miserable, she went straight into Mark's arms and refused to let him put her down again.

It turned out that Payton—who they found curled on her bed asleep—was also running a slight fever, and complained that her throat was also sore.

"Jamie's been a little quieter than usual, too," Mrs. McSwaim told Miranda. "Kasey said he feels okay, but I wouldn't be surprised if they all got sick. That's how it goes with kids, usually. Once one of them catches something, it gets them all."

"What do you suppose it is? Should we call a doctor?"

"I talked to one of the mothers from Payton's preschool. Turns out there's a virus going around. Nothing serious, just a bad cold, basically. Since antibiotics do more harm than good when it comes to viruses, the doctors simply recommend plenty of fluids and over-the-counter medicines to control the symptoms—unless they take a dramatic turn for the worse, of course."

"Of course," Miranda repeated weakly.

Mrs. McSwaim left a short while later. The rest of the day passed in a blur of tears and runny noses. While Mark did his best to keep the children entertained, Miranda filled endless cups of juice and water, then prepared cans of chicken-noodle soup for an early dinner—which reminded her that she had never gotten around to eating lunch. Neither had Mark. They had spent their lunch break rolling around on the floor of her old apartment.

But no. She wasn't going to think of that, she reminded herself, setting bowls and spoons on the kitchen table.

Madison wouldn't let go of her father even long enough to eat, so Mark sat her in his lap and pretty much fed her dinner. Studying her flushed little face and glassy eyes, Miranda couldn't really blame him for pampering her. The child looked so small and miserable.

They moved back into the den after dinner, promising the children a video before bedtime. Mark settled into his recliner with Madison, while Jamie climbed onto the couch and Kasey curled on the rug with Poochie.

Miranda was tempted to escape to her room, but it hardly seemed fair to leave Mark with the kids. Instead she sat in a chair in one corner of the room with a book, prepared to provide assistance if necessary. Opening the book, she cast another glance around the room to make sure everyone was settled before she lost herself in the novel.

She noticed Payton standing nearby, looking at her father and sister with tears trickling slowly down her cheek and her lower lip quivering. "Payton? What's wrong?"

Payton looked around dolefully. "I don't feel good, either."

Miranda closed her book. "I know you don't. Is there anything I can do for you?"

Payton looked back at her father, then turned fully to Miranda. "Can I sit in your lap?"

"Oh. Well…sure. I guess so."

Payton climbed into the large wingchair and squirmed into position in Miranda's lap. The movement caught Mark's attention. He looked away from Madison with a frown. "Payton—"

"It's okay, Mark. She can sit here for a little while if she wants to."

He nodded and turned back to his younger daughter, but Miranda noted that he looked a bit concerned. Was he worried that Payton was being a nuisance? Or was there some other reason he didn't want them getting too cozy?

Payton snuggled into her shoulder. "You smell good," she murmured. "Like flowers."

"Thank you."

"When can I get my ears pierced?"

"That's not up to me," Miranda reminded her with an amused smile. This kid certainly took advantage of every opportunity. "You'll have to ask your father."

Payton sighed gustily. "He'll just say no again."

"Then you'll have to wait until he says yes."

"Maybe you could tell him all girls wear earrings. He probably doesn't know."

"He knows. He's just not ready for you to grow up too quickly," Miranda replied quietly.

"You think he'll ever let me go on a date?"

Miranda was startled into a laugh. "*How* old are you?"

"Four-going-on-five. Nicola said she's going on a date when she's twelve. You think I can go on a date when I'm twelve?"

"Let's just say I'm beginning to understand why your father looks so worried sometimes."

"Shh," Madison chided from Mark's lap. Sending a frown their way, she pointed a chubby finger at the television. "Movie."

Mark reminded Madison about her manners, but Payton's attention had turned toward the video now. Curling her feet beneath her on Miranda's lap, she sat quietly and watched. It wasn't long before her deepening breathing let Miranda know that she had fallen asleep.

Miranda looked around the room again. Kasey was watching the TV intently, petting a blissful Poochie's ears at the same time. Jamie's eyelids were beginning to droop visibly as he lay on the couch, fighting to stay awake. Madison was also on the verge of sleep, one finger in her mouth as she lay back against Mark's arm.

Whee, Miranda couldn't help thinking. Another exciting Saturday night in her new life. Sitting in a chair with a sick child in her lap, surrounded by other sick kids, watching an animated, talking fish swim across a large-screen TV. She thought of her friends at various clubs and parties around town, and she knew they would be appalled at the very thought of such a sedate Saturday evening.

Carefully she shifted Payton's weight to relieve the pressure on her chest. But, unfortunately, not even that change in position helped.

By the time the video ended, Kasey was the only child awake to watch it. His left arm numb from the shoulder down, Mark held his heavily sleeping younger daughter and took a quick survey of the others.

His gaze lingered on Miranda. Still holding Payton, she seemed to be watching the television, but Mark would bet that she had no idea what was taking place on the screen. Her thoughts were obviously far away.

His attention focused on the lines of strain around her mouth. He had always thought of Miranda wearing a perpetual smile, amused at everything around her even when no one else got the joke.

She wasn't smiling now.

In fact, he thought with an ache in his chest, she wore much the same expression his ex-wife had just before she had taken off in search of a more adventurous and exciting life. One that didn't include a man who came irrevocably bound to two vulnerable little girls.

Chapter Thirteen

Mark usually took the girls to church on Sunday mornings, but that was out of the question today, since Madison and Jamie still weren't feeling quite up to par. Payton said she was feeling better, and Kasey showed no signs of catching the virus this time, fortunately. Since there was plenty of time, Mark prepared a nice breakfast of scrambled eggs, crisp bacon and blueberry muffins.

Miranda was the last one into the kitchen. Everyone else was already seated at the table. Though she was fully dressed, she looked a bit harried when she came in. "I'm sorry. I overslept."

And yet she didn't look as though she had slept well at all, Mark decided, discreetly studying the purple smudges beneath her eyes that her makeup could not quite conceal. "Don't worry about it. We don't have any specific plans for the day."

"You made this nice breakfast. I'll clean up afterward."

He shrugged slightly to indicate that he wouldn't argue with her. "Help yourself to coffee or juice—whatever you like."

She stopped first by Jamie's chair, resting a hand on the boy's forehead. "You still feel a bit warm."

"I feel better," Jamie assured her, anxious, as always, not to cause her any concern.

She smiled and patted his shoulder. "I'm sure you'll be back to normal in no time. How do you feel, Payton?"

"I feel better, too. Will you paint my fingernails red like yours?"

"Maybe we'll find a pretty pink, if that's okay with your dad."

"Sure," Mark replied, figuring nail paint was preferable to earlobe punctures. "If Miss Martin has time."

Carrying a cup of coffee, Miranda took her seat at the table. "I'll make time. I'd also like to get some lists made today—everything I need to do this week in preparation for our move."

"When are we going to move, Aunt 'Randa?" Kasey asked.

"As soon as we can. I bet Madison would love to have her bedroom back—and you two are going to have a new room of your own."

From what Mark could tell, Kasey had no problem with the prospect of moving. He knew the boys had moved frequently with their mother, so maybe Kasey simply didn't expect to stay in any one place for long.

Jamie, he noted, looked less enthusiastic—but perhaps that could be attributed to the fact that he still wasn't feeling well.

"Is there a swimming pool?" Kasey wanted to know.

"A nice, big swimming pool," Miranda assured him. "And a playground with swings and a jungle gym."

"Can I come swim and play on the playground?" Payton asked, worried that she was being left out of the plans.

"You will be welcome to visit us," Miranda replied without looking at Mark.

Mark reached over to wipe Madison's runny nose with a tissue. Miranda wasn't the only one who hadn't slept well. He had lain awake trying to come to terms with the fact that she was going to move out and go on with her life.

He had known all along that she would, he reminded himself. Wasn't that why he'd kept telling himself not to get too involved with her? Not that he'd paid the least attention to his own advice.

He had waded in without hesitation, opening his home—and his heart—to her. What kind of masochist was he, that he kept letting himself care for the wrong people? He could only hope that Payton and Madison hadn't had time to become too fond of Miranda and the twins. Maybe his would be the only heart that was bruised this time.

* * *

It was midafternoon before Miranda got around to painting Payton's fingernails—and toenails, too, while she was at it. "Be still, kiddo, or you're going to make me mess this up. You want pink polish on your ankles?"

"Oh. Sorry." Holding her little painted fingers fanned out beside her, Payton stopped wiggling her feet.

Wearing a brightly patterned T-shirt and khaki shorts, Miranda sat cross-legged on the den floor, bent over the chubby little toes she was decorating. She had spread a towel on the floor between them, just in case there were any accidents with the bright pink enamel. "You'll have to wear sandals to school tomorrow so everyone can see your pedicure."

"What's a peddy-cure?"

"A manicure for your feet. Remember I told you what a manicure is?"

Payton nodded, watching the tiny brush intently. "That's a pretty pink. I like your red, too."

"The pink's better at your age. Goes better with your blond hair and blue eyes, anyway."

Payton batted her long lashes. "My daddy said I have bee-yoo-tiful eyes."

"Your daddy is right. But be careful not to act too conceited about it. Every time you pay yourself a compliment, you get just a little less pretty."

"Really?"

"To other people it seems that way. Don't you know kids who brag all the time about how great they are?"

"Jessica Green. She always thinks she's better than *everyone* else."

"And do you enjoy being around her?"

"Yuck. No."

"There you go. She lost her appeal to you because she's too full of herself."

"So, even if you think you're the best at something, you shouldn't say so, right?"

"I'm sure your daddy has told you that before."

"I guess so."

"That's what I thought." Miranda leaned back to admire her handiwork. "There. All the little piggies are painted. When they're dry, you can go show your dad."

"But I can't tell him how pretty I look?" Payton asked with a frown.

"No. You let him say it. And then you give him a flirty smile and say, 'Aren't you sweet to say that?' Trust me, you can use that trick for the rest of your life."

Jamie looked around from a card game he and Kasey were playing on the carpet nearby. "That looks good, Payton," he said, polite as always.

She beamed at him, fluttered those impossibly long lashes, and said charmingly, "Well, aren't you sweet?"

She then turned to Miranda. "Like that?"

Miranda blinked. "Um—yeah. I think you've got it down." Even Jamie looked a bit dazed.

She felt a tap on her shoulder. She was surprised to see Madison standing there. Shy Madison usually avoided her. "What is it, Maddie? Do you need something?"

The little girl held out her hands. "My turn."

"You want me to paint your fingernails?"

Madison nodded. "Pink."

"Oh. Okay." She supposed it would be all right with Mark. "But you can't put your fingers in your mouth until they're dry."

"'Kay." Madison settled on the carpet next to Payton and stuck out her hands.

Smiling, Miranda cradled one little hand carefully in hers and applied the brush. Their heads were very close together as they bent over the task. As tiny as the brush was, it still completely covered Madison's little nails in one swipe.

Madison looked up and gave Miranda a bright smile. "Pretty."

Darn it, now she had a lump in her throat. She swallowed and murmured, "Yes, Madison. Very pretty."

A faint sound from the doorway made her glance in that direction. Mark was standing there, watching them with an expression that made her heart race.

She should make a clever remark to break the tension, but her mind had gone completely blank when their eyes met across the room. Fortunately Payton was never at a loss for words.

"Daddy!" she all but shrieked. "Look what Miranda did. She said I could call her that."

Pulling his gaze away from Miranda, Mark smiled down at his daughter, who was waving her hands in front of him. "You look very pretty."

"Aren't you sweet?"

Mark chuckled. "Who's been giving you Southern belle lessons?"

"Miranda," Payton replied promptly.

Miranda shrugged when Mark looked at her. "I hope you don't mind, but Madison wanted her nails painted, too."

"Very nice, Maddie."

The child nodded. "I'm pretty, too."

Miranda almost sighed. Neither of Mark's girls suffered from a lack of self-esteem, apparently.

She was blowing on Madison's fingernails to help them dry more quickly, and eliciting a burst of giggles in response, when the doorbell rang.

Judging from Mark's curious expression, he hadn't been expecting anyone. He turned to go answer the door, leaving Miranda to convince Madison that she didn't really need her toenails painted. But Madison simply extended her bare feet in front of Miranda's face and wiggled her toes expectantly. If Payton's toes were painted, Madison wanted hers to be, too.

Resigned, Miranda bent over the task, warning Madison that she would have to be still until the polish dried. The small girl agreed contentedly.

Miranda had just applied polish to the last little piggy when Mark returned to the den, followed by a couple Miranda had never seen before. Replacing the cap on the polish, she smiled at the newcomers, who appeared to be in their mid-to late-thirties, though she had never been good at guessing ages.

The woman was a petite strawberry-blonde with

wide-set green eyes and a smattering of golden freckles over fair skin that was still firm and smooth except for a few smile lines she'd made no effort to hide. Miranda's gaze lingered appreciatively for a moment on the handsome cowboy who accompanied the woman. Tousled dark hair, narrowed blue eyes, a tan that hadn't been acquired in a booth. A long, lean body encased in a denim shirt, well-worn jeans, and work-scuffed boots. Nice.

Spotting her on the floor, he smiled, and she felt her pulse rate accelerate slightly in response. Oh, yeah. Very nice.

Mark made the introductions as Miranda rose to her feet. "Miranda Martin, I'd like you to meet Shane Walker and his wife—I'm sorry, is it Kelly?"

The woman nodded, not looking at all offended that Mark had almost forgotten her name. Because it seemed uncharacteristic, Miranda glanced at him curiously. Mark was definitely rattled, she decided. Something about these unexpected visitors had obviously caught him off guard.

"These are my daughters, Payton and Madison," Mark continued, motioning to each as he spoke. "And Miranda's nephews. Kascy—" Kasey nodded to indicate that Mark had correctly pointed him out. "And Jamie."

Shane smiled at the boys. "Twins run in my family, too. I have two uncles who are identical twins, and no one can ever tell them apart. And one of my uncles has twin sons of his own."

"Do you and Kelly have children, Shane?" Mark asked. Miranda decided he was making innocuous conversation to give himself time to recover from the surprise of finding this couple—whoever they were—at his doorstep.

Shane smiled proudly. "Like you, we have two girls. Annie's seven and Lucy is four."

"Did they come with you?" Payton asked eagerly.

"They're at my aunt's house tonight," Shane replied. "But I'm sure they would love to meet you sometime."

"Payton, why don't you take Madison and the boys and go have a snack while I talk to my visitors?" Mark suggested, his voice still sounding a bit strained to Miranda. "I'm sure you can find something in the kitchen."

"I'll get them settled," Miranda offered, motioning the children toward the doorway. "May I get any of you anything? There's a fresh pitcher of iced tea."

"I'd like some tea, if it's not too much trouble," Shane accepted.

"I'll bring some for everyone." With one last, searching glance at Mark, Miranda followed the children to the kitchen.

Sitting with his guests in the now-quiet den, Mark studied Shane Walker with a renewed sense of disbelief at the unexpected visit. Although it had been almost fifteen years since he had seen Shane, he had recognized him as soon as he had opened the door. The good-looking teenager had grown into a handsome man who bore an almost uncanny resemblance to his dad, Jared Walker—Mark's long-ago foster father.

"I'm really surprised to see you," he said, though he was sure Shane had already assumed as much.

"I know we should have called before we showed up at your doorstep, but it seemed too complicated to explain over the telephone. I figured it would be easier to talk face to face."

"Shane has always believed in taking shortcuts," Kelly said with a shake of her head. "I told him we should call."

"No, it's fine. So, how did you find me?"

"Maybe I should tell you *why* we found you first," Shane answered.

Mark nodded. "I'm listening."

Before Shane could speak again, Miranda returned carrying a tray holding glasses of iced tea and a plate of Mrs. McSwaim's homemade cookies. She served the drinks, set the cookies on the coffee table, and asked, "Can I get you anything else?"

"We're fine." Mark patted the couch beside him. "Have a seat, Miranda. The kids will come get us if they need us."

She looked uncertain about joining them, as if concerned that she was intruding.

"Please join us," Kelly seconded with a warm smile. "We can all have a nice visit."

"You remember I told you about the ranch where I stayed the year my mother was ill?" Mark prodded when Miranda took a seat beside him.

"Yes, I remember. Outside of Dallas, right?"

He nodded. "Shane's parents own that ranch. He was a college student the year I was there, but he came home nearly every weekend to help out around the ranch."

"I never actually wanted to go to college," Shane admitted in his deep drawl. "My dad and stepmother insisted. I majored in business, but I never aspired to do anything but run the ranch with Dad."

"So you're still there?" Miranda asked.

"Yep. Kelly and I have a house next to Dad and Cassie's. We still raise horses and a few cattle, and we still take in at-risk teenagers. We have a social worker on staff now, in addition to Dad, Cassie, Kelly and me. We usually have between five and eight boys at a time in residence."

Mark raised his eyebrows. "There were only one or two boys at a time when I was there."

Shane nodded. "We just became a full-time residential facility about five years ago, after Dad finally admitted that he was as interested in training kids as he was horses."

Mark thought of the quiet-spoken, work-toughened man he had both feared and idolized during his stay at the ranch. "Your father and stepmother are well, then?"

"Oh, yeah. Dad can still outwork me any day and Cassie's still a bundle of nonstop energy."

"And your little sister? Molly. She must be—what? College age now?"

Shane chuckled. "Molly's twenty-four. She's been out of college for a couple of years."

"Hard to imagine. What's she doing now?"

"Actually Molly's the reason I'm here," Shane said, getting down to business. "She wanted me to find you."

Mark was now thoroughly confused. "*Molly* wanted you to find me?"

Shane's much-younger half-sister had been a red-haired moppet the last time Mark had seen her, and he had barely known her. Jared had not encouraged his foster boys to spend much time with his pampered and protected daughter. Still, it had been hard to live at the ranch for more than a few days without getting to know Molly at least a little, since she had seemed to be everywhere at once, chattering and asking questions and begging to bc included.

Shane nodded, his firm mouth tilting into a lopsided smile. "I don't know if you remember, but Molly has always had a knack for getting what she wants."

"And what is it she wants from me?" Mark asked a bit warily.

"She has decided she wants to throw a big surprise party for Dad and Cassie's twenty-fifth wedding anniversary in October. She wants all of Dad and Cassie's favorite foster sons to be there. There are a few we haven't heard from in several years, so I'm not sure she'll have everyone there, but I told her I would help out as much as possible. When I learned that you live here in Little Rock, I promised her I would contact you while I'm here for a visit with my aunt Lindsay and her husband."

"How *did* you find me?" Mark asked curiously. He

had made no effort to hide from his past, but he had no ties left with anyone in Texas. He'd lived in Arkansas for nearly six years now, since he'd accepted a job with a large Little Rock accounting firm.

"I have three uncles who own a private investigation agency in Dallas," Shane explained. "They specialize in finding people—reuniting families, locating biological parents for adoptees, that sort of thing. They have a division that offers corporate security consultations, but they're best known for finding people. Not that you were all that hard to find, since you have a Web page for your accounting business—with your photograph on it. I recognized you as soon as I saw your picture."

Mark shook his head in amazement. "I wasn't trying to hide. I just never expected to hear from anyone from that stage of my life."

"I understand if your memories of that time are unhappy ones. Your mother was very ill, wasn't she? I remember you were anxious to get back to her so you could take care of her and your little sister."

"You remember that?"

"Of course," Shane answered simply. "I remember you very well, Mark. I guess I always identified with you because I'd have felt the same way if anyone had tried to take me away from Cassie and Molly. Especially if I thought they needed me."

Mark was absurdly pleased that Shane remembered him that well. He'd had a slight case of hero worship for Shane back then, convinced that Shane could do anything. Ride, rope, play sports, charm every female within sight of his lethal dimples. Mark had wanted to grow up to be just like Shane. Except for the cowboy part.

"My memories of the ranch are not bad ones," he felt obligated to say. "Except for my concern about my mother and sister, I was happy there. I always felt rather guilty about not keeping in touch, but it upset my mother too badly to be reminded of the time we had to be apart. She died a few years later, and then it just seemed too late to make contact again."

"That makes sense. But I know Dad and Cassie would really like to see you, if you can come. You were always special to them. Cassie said you had the biggest heart of any of her boys."

"He hasn't changed a bit," Miranda murmured beside him.

He slanted her a look. He wasn't sure how he felt about hearing that the Walkers remembered him fondly after all these years. He had been in the habit of thinking himself pretty much alone in the present, completely disconnected from his past except for his sporadic contact with his globe-trotting sister. He had never considered revisiting his youth—and he wasn't entirely sure he wanted to.

"I brought you a letter from Molly giving you all the details." Shane set a sealed white envelope on the coffee table. "We'll understand, of course, if you can't come, but we all hope you can make it."

"Your children might enjoy a visit to the ranch,"

Kelly added. "We'll have games and tours and horse-back riding going on all weekend."

Payton would love that, Mark reflected. So would the boys, actually—not that he expected to be involved in their lives in October, which was still five months away.

Looking to his future was almost as depressing as looking backward.

Shane spoke again. "If you can't come, but you have a special memory of your time on the ranch—or if you feel that your stay there benefited you in some way since—Molly would appreciate you sending a note to her about it. I think she's making a memory book."

"If I can't come, I will definitely send a letter," Mark agreed. That seemed like a small enough favor for the people who had once been so kind to him.

"You would be welcome to bring guests, of course," Kelly said, smiling at Miranda. "There is always room at the ranch for new friends—and especially room for extra children."

Both Mark and Miranda merely smiled noncommittally. Mark could not even say whether he would make the trip to the ranch. He couldn't begin to guess what Miranda thought of the open invitation.

Shane glanced at his watch. "We'd better be going. I promised Aunt Lindsay we would be back in time for dinner."

"I remember your aunt Lindsay, I think." Mark had a vague mental picture of a pretty, brown-haired, blue-eyed woman. "She's married to a doctor, isn't she?"

"Nick Grant," Shane confirmed with a nod. "They visited the ranch several times while you were there. Along with my father's other four siblings and their families, of course."

"Your father is one of six siblings?" Miranda asked, mentally doing the math.

"Seven, actually. One died in his teens. They were orphaned young, separated and sent into foster homes. The youngest two were adopted—Aunt Michelle and Aunt Lindsay. They were all adults when they were finally reunited more than twenty years ago."

"They're an extremely close family now," Kelly added. "No matter how many newcomers join them, they are always greeted with open arms and open hearts. That's the way it was for me when I met them all."

Shane gave his wife a loving smile before glancing back at Mark. "That's why my dad takes in at-risk boys—because of his own past. Lindsay and Nick take in foster kids, too."

"Foster kids?"

The words were repeated in a shocked, high-pitched voice. Mark looked around to the doorway, as did the other adults.

Kasey and Jamie stood there, staring at Miranda with stricken faces. Mark wasn't sure which boy had spoken, but they looked equally upset.

"You said we didn't have to go to a foster home." Mark thought it was Kasey who made the accusation to Miranda. "You said we could stay with you."

Jamie stood mutely beside his brother, his lower lip quivering, tears tracking down his cheeks.

Miranda jumped to her feet and hurried toward the boys. "We weren't talking about you guys. Mr. Walker was telling us about his aunt."

"He said she takes foster kids. You're going to send us to her, aren't you?"

"No." Miranda knelt in front of them, her expression almost fierce. "I'm not sending you away, Kasey. I gave you my word that you can stay with me, and I'm not going to take it back. You really did walk in while we were talking about something that had nothing to do with you two. I promise."

"She's right, boys," Mark seconded, moving to stand behind her. "We were actually talking about *me*. Mr. Walker's parents were my foster family a long time ago when my mother got sick and couldn't take care of me. That's why he came to visit me—just to catch up with an old friend."

Jamie's breath hitched. "We can still stay with you, Aunt 'Randa?"

"Absolutely," she assured him. "We're going to move into our new apartment next week and we'll get along just fine together. We're family, Jamie."

The boy's eyes filled again. "Mama is family, and she went away."

Mark watched as Miranda's cheeks paled. He felt his own throat tighten. He knew Shane and Kelly were watching with expressions of sympathy; they had probably figured out the situation by now. It must have looked like a familiar enough scene to them, considering their experience with children separated from their biological parents for a multitude of reasons.

Miranda gathered a twin in each arm and gave them a hug. It was the first time Mark had seen her do so.

"I am not sending you away," she told them firmly. "Is that clear?"

Both boys hugged her back, Jamie clinging to her neck. They seemed to be convinced, finally, and immeasurably relieved. After a moment, she sent them back to the kitchen, promising to join them very soon.

As soon as they were out of hearing, she turned to Shane. "You said your uncles specialize in locating missing people?"

"Yes. I have three uncles and a cousin in that business."

"Would you mind leaving me a phone number for them? There's someone I really need to find."

Chapter Fourteen

Mark waited until after all the children were in bed before confronting Miranda. He suspected it had been her intention to slip off to bed without having a private conversation with him, but he'd caught her in the kitchen filling a glass with water. "Are you sure it's a good idea to hire someone to look for your sister?"

"I need to find her," Miranda said, her expression a mixture of defensiveness and stubbornness. "The boys deserve to know where their mother is, and whether she's all right."

"You think she'll take them back if you find her? That she'll be in a position to do so, even if she wants to?"

Miranda set the glass down with such a hard thump

that water splashed over her hand and the counter. She looked genuinely annoyed when she snapped, "I am *not* trying to get rid of the twins. I simply want to find my sister."

"She asked you not to try to find her. She implied that you could put her in danger if you did so."

"I'll explain that to Shane's uncle when I talk to him. Surely a trained P.I. will know how to handle a situation like this."

"Maybe."

"What would you do if it were your sister?" she challenged him. "If she suddenly disappeared, leaving only a cryptic note? Something tells me you'd have started looking a lot sooner than I have."

"Maybe," he said again.

"You know you would. The only reason it has taken me this long is that I was so stunned at first, and I had the boys to worry about. I just need to know she's okay. And maybe I need to be convinced she isn't going to just show up on my doorstep and take the boys away after I've rearranged my whole life—and theirs."

"So you want to keep them?"

"I want what's best for them," she replied wearily, her momentary flash of temper cooling now. "They shouldn't have to worry all the time about being sent to foster homes, or never knowing where they're going to be living."

Mark studied her face for a moment. "I said once that you loved them, and you didn't seem to know how to respond. I think you know how you feel about them now."

"I do love them. How could I not? They're amazing kids."

"They are special," he agreed, "which isn't to say there won't be problems with them as they get older and more sure of themselves."

"I'm aware of that. It makes me nervous, but I guess I can deal with it—I have no choice, really, do I?"

"You don't have to deal with it alone."

His quiet words made Miranda back instinctively against the counter behind her. She couldn't know, of course, that the words had startled him almost as much as they had her.

She forced a bright smile that looked completely fake. "You've offered your assistance any time I need it. That's very generous of you. You're a good friend."

"Surely you know by now that I want to be a lot more than a friend to you," he said roughly. He hadn't actually intended to get into this tonight, but she seemed poised on the verge of flight at any moment. He wasn't sure he would have another chance.

"I told you I can't deal with this now." There was an edge of panic in her voice.

"I know you did. And I will give you time, but I guess I feel the way you do about needing some answers, Miranda. I'd like to know that when you leave here, you won't be cutting me out of your life without a backward look. I need to know you're going to give us a chance."

"I'll be very busy for a while," she said, avoiding his gaze, "settling into the new apartment, taking care of work and the boys—"

"Damn it, you *are* looking for excuses."

Her temper flared again. "Maybe I'm just not interested. Have you considered that?"

"I've considered it," he replied coolly. "And then I remember what it was like when we made love at your apartment, and I know better."

Her cheeks pinkened, and he could almost see the sensual memories swirling within her amber eyes. "That was just a one-time thing. A way to blow off some steam."

He took a step closer to her, his eyes locked with hers now. "So you keep trying to convince me. I don't believe it—and I don't think you do, either."

"You hardly even know me."

"I've known you for a year," he countered, moving a step closer. "And I've wanted you almost that long."

"There's a physical attraction—"

"It's a hell of a lot more than that." He brought his hands up and captured her face between them. "I'm crazy about you, Miranda Martin. I have been for months. And what's more, you've known it."

She moistened her lips with the tip of her tongue, and though it seemed to be a subconscious action on her part, it made his gut clench. His gaze focused hungrily on her glistening lips when she said, "I knew there was…something. But I told you, I don't get involved with men with kids. It's too complicated."

He couldn't resist brushing a kiss against the end of her nose. "Circumstances have changed since then."

She wasn't trying to push him away, but she wasn't

pulling him closer, either. She stood very still, her face pale, her pulse fluttering visibly in her throat. "You're right," she conceded. "Now there are four kids who can be hurt if you and I try something foolish and then make a mess of it. I can't be responsible for four kids, Mark. It's taking all the courage I have just to keep the boys."

"I take full responsibility for my girls. But there's no reason any of the children should be hurt, as long as you and I are mature and discreet. I happen to think we have a lot to offer all of them, you and I. The boys need a man's presence in their life, and my girls were delighted to have someone around to paint their fingernails."

Miranda's breathing had taken on a slight gasping sound, as though she were having trouble getting air. "I can't do this now," she whispered. "It's just too much."

He wanted to argue—but he couldn't stand seeing her looking so distressed. With a gusty sigh of regret, he conceded defeat—for now. "I'm not going to push you into something you aren't ready for," he promised. "But could I ask you one question?"

She eyed him warily. "What?"

"Are my girls the only reason you're so reluctant to get involved with me?"

"They're...the biggest reason," she admitted after a moment. "They're great kids, and I am terrified of doing anything that would be detrimental to them."

"And the other reasons?" he prodded, sensing there was more.

She shrugged somewhat helplessly. "I've never wanted to get too involved with *anyone.* I like being on my own, answerable to no one. I like making my own decisions, setting my own hours, making my own plans."

"You're thinking of your parents. Surely you know I'm nothing like your domineering father. I want an equal partner in my life, Miranda, not a submissive companion." He wanted what he had seen between Shane and Kelly—and he knew now that he wanted it with Miranda.

"You're nothing like my father," she admitted after a brief hesitation. "You're a genuinely good man, Mark. I think you would give me the shirt off your back, if I asked you to. I've never met anyone more generous or unselfish or kindhearted."

He scowled and dropped his arms to his sides. "I'm not a freaking saint, Miranda."

"Maybe not a saint, but you do seem to specialize in taking care of people. When you think someone needs your help, you would do anything for him—or her."

Comprehension slammed into him with the force of a blow to his head. "You think I see you as some sort of charity case?" he asked incredulously.

"I didn't say that, exactly…"

He swore beneath his breath, and though she looked surprised by his uncharacteristic language, he didn't bother to apologize. He was the one who was annoyed now. Actually "annoyed" wasn't a strong enough word.

"I really don't appreciate you acting as though I'm

an idiot," he snapped. "I'm not a giant sucker who falls for any hard-luck story, and I don't have a superhero complex. I have no compulsion to rush to the rescue of every damsel in distress I see."

"I didn't—"

He was on a roll now, and he didn't give her a chance to explain. "Yes, I made a mistake when I married Brooke for all the wrong reasons. I was young and infatuated, and I misjudged my feelings for her, and the kind of person she was. I don't regret that mistake too badly, because I have my daughters as a result of that marriage. But I'm thirty years old now, and I would like to think I've learned a few things about life—and about myself—since then."

"Still—"

He wasn't quite finished. "If you'll remember, you weren't in any sort of a fix when I asked you out to dinner. You were cruising along very well financially and professionally, totally independent and happy with your life. I admired that immensely. You didn't seem to need me—or anyone—but I still asked you out. It was something I had been wanting to do for months. Does that sound as though I thought of you as a charity case?"

"No," she admitted.

"Damn straight." He nodded in satisfaction. "I've been pleased to be able to help you out since your nephews arrived, Miranda, but that has nothing to do with my feelings for you. I fell hard for you a long time ago, and as far as I'm concerned, the boys are just a nice part of the total package."

Her lashes swept downward, hiding the expression in her eyes. "So maybe I was wrong about your reasons—"

"You were most definitely wrong."

"But I'm not wrong about *my* feelings," she continued stubbornly. "And I'm not ready for this, Mark. I'm sorry, but I'm just not."

He paused, then sighed. "And if I continue to push you, I really will be as bad as your controlling father," he said in resignation. "Do what you need to do—but I hope you won't shut me out of your life without at least giving us a chance."

"I—" She crossed her arms over her chest, looking atypically vulnerable—and very far away, even though they still stood quite close. "Maybe we can have dinner or something, once the boys and I are settled."

It wasn't enough—not nearly enough—to satisfy him, but it would have to do for now.

He nodded. "I'll continue to help you in any way I can—not because I think of you as a charity case, but because I care about you and the boys. And while I can't promise to keep all my feelings about you to myself, I will try to give you the time you need to decide how you feel about me."

Looking downward, she nodded.

He told himself to move away, but he found himself reaching out for her, instead. "Because I'm really not a saint…"

He was gratified that she lifted her mouth to his when he lowered his head.

Just in case it would be a while before he could kiss her again, he made the most of this embrace. He took his time savoring her soft lips before he slipped his tongue between them. His entire body ached for more, but he limited himself to no more than this lingering, emotionally charged kiss.

When he finally drew back, her lips clung to his until he reluctantly broke the contact. Her eyelids were heavy, her cheeks flushed, her breathing unsteady when she gazed up at him. She was definitely not immune to him, but he was well aware of how stubborn she could be when she thought she was protecting her precious independence.

"That was just to hold me over," he murmured huskily, making himself release her. "Good night, Miranda."

To give him credit, Mark kept his word not to pressure her during the next few days. Not that she should be surprised, she thought. Though not quite a saint— as he had proven during a kiss that had all but melted her from the inside out—he was still the most honorable man she had ever known. He had given his word and she trusted him. Mostly.

Even had he wanted something more to happen between them, there was no opportunity. Miranda was so busy she hardly had a moment to breathe. She enrolled the boys in a day-care center, signed the lease on the apartment she had selected, made arrangements for a moving company, took care of changing her utilities and billing addresses. And somehow she continued to do her job, working eight and nine hours a day, skipping lunches so she wouldn't be late getting home.

She told herself she was staying busy because she had so much to do. But part of her was well aware that her frantic schedule gave her an excuse to avoid any more intimate talks with Mark.

Sometimes she caught him looking at her in a way that told her he was remembering their kisses. Their lovemaking. And every time, her heart stopped as the memories flooded her mind, too. Each time she thought of their conversation in the kitchen, she was forced to throw herself into another burst of activity to ward off a full-blown panic attack.

He had all but said that he was in love with her. He had told her flat-out that he was interested in more than a casual dating relationship with her. Mark was the marriage-and-family type. The fact that he had failed once at the attempt didn't change his basic nature.

And she—well, she was the love 'em and leave 'em type. At least, she had always aspired to be, even if she hadn't exactly lived up to that image in the past.

She hadn't expected to fall in love with Mr. Respectability.

Just the thought of the L word had her packing like a crazy woman again. Anything to keep herself too busy to think about Mark Wallace.

She moved out the following Saturday. It didn't help that Payton and Madison cried when they realized

Miranda and the boys would no longer be living in their house.

Miranda still felt like a heel when she and Mark carried the last suitcases into her new apartment, having left the sniffling girls with Mrs. McSwaim. The movers had already brought her furniture and a delivery crew had set up the bunk beds and dressers she had purchased for the boys, so except for a few hours' worth of unpacking, they were all moved in.

Leaving the boys to start putting away their clothes, Miranda joined Mark in the living room. It was another small apartment, but the two bedrooms and two tiny bathrooms made it much more functional for three.

Mark glanced at the bare white walls. "I guess you'll be glad when you get your framed posters hung. Right now this place looks much too colorless for your taste."

She nodded. "It will feel more like home once I've decorated."

For now, it felt rather cold and sterile. She told herself that soon she would feel as comfortable here as she had in her former apartment. Or in Mark's house.

Which reminded her...

"I'm sorry the girls were so upset when we left. I never meant to cause them any distress. I should have stayed where I was until I found this place, rather than turning your household upside down."

"Sleeping on the sofa? Sharing a single bathroom with a couple of boys? I think it was better all around the way we handled it. The girls enjoyed having you all there, but they'll readjust quickly. Kids do at that age."

Miranda wished the same were true for adults. She wasn't at all sure she would adjust so easily. And the brooding expression Mark had worn all day told her that he wouldn't, either. But they *would* recover, eventually, she assured herself. With hearts intact, preferably, thanks to her refusal to be swept into an impetuous love affair.

"So, do you need me to help you unpack or hang pictures or anything?"

"No, the boys and I can handle it from here. We have all weekend—and it's not like there's that much more to do. It was definitely worth the cost to hire the movers."

He nodded and stuffed his hands into the pockets of his jeans. "Well…I guess I'd better get back to the girls, then. You'll call if you need anything?"

"Yes, I will. But I'm sure we'll be fine."

He sighed heavily. "I have no doubt that you will be."

She didn't know what to say.

Pulling his hands free, he took a step toward the door. "Tell the boys I'll see them later, okay?"

"Mark—" Impulse had her moving toward him, resting a hand on his arm. "Thank you. For everything."

His brows drew down into a scowl. "Don't treat this like goodbye. It's not."

Not goodbye—but it would be different now. She saw no need to point that out, since it had to be as obvious to him as it was to her. "I just want to make sure you understand how grateful I am for all you did."

"Yeah. I know. I'm a great guy. A real pal."

She had never heard him sound bitter before. She didn't like it. "Mark—"

He shook his head, his smile twisting. "You know what occurred to me last night? There's one question I've forgotten to ask myself too many times before I dive into something."

She wasn't following him. "I don't—"

He seemed to be talking to himself almost. "Maybe I should start asking that question before I reach out to anyone again."

"What question?"

He looked at her with a jumbled mixture of emotions seething in his eyes. "What's in it for *me?*"

A few moments later, he was gone, the apartment door closing with an angry snap behind him.

"Aunt 'Randa? Where's Mark? Did he leave?"

She glanced around numbly, unable to force a smile even for the boys' sake. "Yes. He left."

Jamie sighed wistfully. "I'll miss him," he murmured with the fatalism of someone who had grown accustomed to saying goodbye.

Miranda rested a hand on his shoulder. "So will I," she murmured. "So will I."

But she still had her freedom, she reminded herself. Her precious independence. No one told her what to do. Ever. No one criticized her or found fault with her or hurt her by treating her as if she were unworthy of love or respect. Her parents had done all those things to her.

A tiny voice inside her reminded her that Mark had done none of them.

She drowned out that insidious little voice with her own. "Come on, guys," she said briskly, turning away from the door. "Let's have a snack and then finish getting our new home in order."

What's in it for me? The question haunted Miranda during the night as she lay in her old bed in her new bedroom, unable to sleep.

The cynical question had been so unlike Mark. As he had pointed out, himself, it was a question he never asked before he reached out to help anyone.

It had, however, been the motivation for Miranda's own behavior since she had left her parents' home. Taking in her nephews was probably the only purely unselfish act she had committed in at least ten years.

Maybe Mark should be more like her, in some ways. Anyone who did as much for other people as Mark did was bound to get hurt. He *had* been hurt, on more than one occasion. And yet he kept reaching out. Opening his heart. Was he incredibly brave, or just a masochist? A fool? Or simply the best man Miranda had ever known?

When it came right down to it, she didn't think he should change at all, she finally decided. Mark Wallace was very close to perfect the way he was. He simply had a bad habit of falling for the wrong women, she reflected sadly.

He deserved better.

Miranda spent all day Sunday unpacking and arranging like crazy, keeping herself too busy to worry about the future. She needed to make the apartment feel like home.

The boys worked contentedly by her side. She had been pleasantly surprised by how much help they had been.

She was a bit dismayed when they unpacked the last of the two big suitcases they had brought with them and she realized how little the twins actually owned. Some jeans and T-shirts, one pair of sneakers each, underwear and pajamas, a very few treasured toys. And that included the die-cast cars that Mark had given them when they'd left his house, letting them choose one each from his collection.

Looking around their spartanly decorated bedroom, she asked, "This is everything?"

The boys nodded.

"Did you have to leave some things behind when you came to me?"

Kasey shrugged. "We had some video games and stuff, but Mama sold it all. She said she needed the money to move to a safe place."

Miranda felt her jaw clench. "You've both been so much help to me that I think we should go do a little shopping later. We'll pick up a couple of extra things to decorate your room. Maybe a video game system."

She would pull out her rarely used credit card, if necessary. While she had no intention of lavishing material possessions on her nephews, they deserved some reward for everything they had been through lately. Especially when they continued to accept each new development with such equanimity.

A knock on her apartment door made her pulse jump.

"I bet that's Mark!" Jamie exclaimed, his face light-ing up. "I hope he brought Payton and Madison. We want to show them our room."

Because Miranda agreed with Jamie's guess about their caller's identity, she took her time getting to the door. She wanted to make sure her expression was calm and composed, though she couldn't resist running a hand through her hair and making sure her cotton shirt and jeans were neat before she opened the door.

But her visitor wasn't Mark, she noted with a mix-ture of disappointment and relief. This was a woman—mid-twenties, choppy dark hair, brilliant blue eyes set in a rather gamine face, a boyish figure in an oversize T-shirt and khakis that were a size too large for her nar-row hips. Yet, Miranda's first impression was of almost delicate femininity—hardly the effect the young woman seemed to be going for.

"Miranda Martin?"

"Yes?"

"I'm B.J. Samples, Shane Walker's cousin. I work for D'Alessandro and Walker Investigations. I tried to call, but your phone isn't connected yet, and the cell phone number I was given directed me to a voice mail system. Mr. Wallace told me where I could find you."

"I just moved in here yesterday, and the phone won't be connected until tomorrow. I meant to keep my cell phone turned on, but I have a bad habit of leav-ing it in my purse and forgetting to check it. Please, come in."

Miranda ushered the woman into her living room.

"The kitchen is still pretty bare, but I have some sodas and juice, I think. May I get you anything?"

"Thank you, no. I'm fine." B.J. perched on the edge of one of Miranda's two mismatched wing chairs. Seeing that the visitor wasn't Mark, the twins disappeared into their bedroom again, leaving Miranda alone with her—who hardly fit the stereotype of the typical private investigator, she couldn't help thinking.

"I certainly didn't expect you to come all the way here from Dallas."

And she couldn't help worrying about how much that trip would cost her. When she had talked to Shane's uncle, Tony D'Alessandro, she had requested that any information they could acquire about her sister be given to her through the mail or a telephone call.

B.J. waved a dismissive hand. "I was in town, anyway. I stopped by to see my aunt Lindsay on my way to St. Louis."

There seemed to be a steady stream of visitors to aunt Lindsay's house, Miranda thought. Must be a fun place to visit. "Are you going to St. Louis on an assignment?"

Miranda thought she detected a gleam of excitement in the other woman's eyes. "Molly—Shane's sister—asked me to try to find another missing foster son and invite him to the party. We aren't sure he's even in St. Louis, but we have a lead that suggests I might find him there."

"You have a fascinating job." Miranda wanted to ask about Lisa, but she found herself stalling with small talk, almost afraid of what she would find out.

B.J. wrinkled her slightly tilted-up nose. "It is when I'm allowed to do anything besides computer searches. I work for three overprotective uncles. I'm lucky when they let me leave the office without a bodyguard. They only sent me on this assignment because everyone else was tied up with other projects, and they figured I couldn't get into too much trouble tracking down a former foster boy."

Miranda drew a deep breath and finally got straight to the point. "Have you found out anything about my sister?"

B.J. reached into the large canvas tote bag she had carried slung over one shoulder. "I have a letter for you. From your sister."

"Did you talk to her? Can you tell me where she is?"

"I can't tell you where she is because I don't know. She moved right after one of my uncles contacted her on your behalf. He handled it very discreetly, but she didn't want to stay where she was after we found her."

Miranda swallowed. "Is she really in the witness protection program?"

B.J. hesitated, then shrugged. "I think it's an unofficial arrangement. She got involved with some pretty shady characters, and it's entirely possible that some of them have a grudge against her for cooperating with prosecutors, but we aren't sure she's in quite as much danger as her original note to you implied."

"I did warn your uncle that Lisa is prone to exaggeration," Miranda murmured, finding some measure of comfort in the information.

"Yes, well, she seems to have a new boyfriend with her now—"

Miranda groaned. "Of course she does."

"—and she made it very clear that she plans to start a new life with him in a new place. She asked us to assure you that she's okay, and to request that you not try to find her again."

"So she really isn't coming back." Miranda had needed to know for sure.

"It doesn't sound like it. I'm sure she explains everything in the letter she sent."

Miranda glanced at the thin envelope she had accepted from B.J. It apparently held no more than a single sheet of paper, probably saying little more than the first letter had.

What was it with these women who could so easily walk away from their children—Mark's ex-wife and now Miranda's sister—leaving other people to deal with the pain they left behind?

She could never do anything like that, she realized. Never. When it had come right down to it, she couldn't even abandon the nephews she had hardly known at the time.

"Miss Martin?" B.J. looked at her searchingly. "Are you okay?"

"Yes. Thanks. I'm just— Thank you," she finished lamely. "I needed to know for certain that my sister was all right. Will your uncle bill me for the agency's services, or should I write you a check?"

B.J. waved a hand again. "No charge. It was a fairly

simple search, really, since my uncle had a few strings he could pull to find your sister rather quickly. And since you're a friend of Mark's—who was like family at one time—Uncle Tony said to tell you it's on the house."

"That really isn't necessary," she exclaimed, shocked by the generous offer. "I never intended—"

"Don't worry about it," B.J. cut in kindly. "They do things like this all the time. Besides, your sister left you and her kids in a tough position. It seemed like the least we could do to help out."

"Thank you," Miranda said again, still a bit bothered by the gesture.

B.J. shook her head. "I can't imagine suddenly being saddled with two little boys. I like kids and all, but that would be one scary proposition."

"It is," Miranda agreed as she escorted B.J. to the door. "But I guess I'm not as scared as I would have thought I'd be."

"Your nephews are lucky that their aunt is the responsible and reliable type, so they had a safe place to go when their mother flaked out on them."

Miranda had already gotten the impression that B.J. said pretty much whatever popped into her mind. Still, she was rather stunned to hear herself referred to as the "responsible and reliable type."

Those were terms she would have applied to Mark, she thought as she closed the door behind the P.I., not to herself. Funny how her self-image was undergoing a radical change from only a few short weeks ago. Perhaps because she was seeing herself through other people's eyes now, rather than as the woman she had always tried to be.

Why had she thought of herself as so much like Lisa? She, who had lived in the same city for several years, who had committed to obtaining a college degree, who had worked for the same company since graduating, and who had believed in putting money aside for the future rather than blowing it all in the present. Even Lisa had always seen her as the responsible one, coming to her when she needed money, sending the twins to her because she had thought Miranda could offer them a more stable home.

Miranda let out a long, gusty breath. Darn it, how had she ended up developing principles? If she had been as blithely self-absorbed as Lisa and Brooke, she could be at a party right now. Flirting, dancing, having fun with no thought of anyone but herself. But no, she had to be "responsible and reliable."

Now she knew exactly why Mark had looked so disgruntled when he had denied being labeled a saint.

Chapter Fifteen

As Miranda had expected, her first week on her own was busy. And a little crazy.

The boys started their day-care program Monday morning. They clung to Miranda when she dropped them off, shy about meeting the other kids and worried what they could expect. But by Wednesday they were looking forward to their day, eagerly telling her about all the activities that were scheduled for them. They were even making a few new friends, though they made them as a pair, neither of the twins straying far from the other.

Miranda was learning how difficult it was to get everyone ready in the morning, put in a whole day's work, do the laundry and the shopping, prepare nutritious dinners and have the boys bathed and in bed at a reasonable hour—only to start all over again the next morning. Her clerical assistant, Stevie Riggs, smiled wryly when Miranda exclaimed about the difficulties.

"Welcome to the world of the average working mother. I wish I could tell you it gets easier, but just wait until the boys are in school and you're trying to juggle teacher conferences and PTA meetings and after-school activities along with the usual routines. Oh, and eventually, one or both of the twins will get sick and you'll either have to find a baby-sitter or miss work."

"Oh, gee. Thanks for the encouragement."

Stevie patted her arm. "You'll get through it somehow. We all do. And if you need moral support, there are quite a few of us here in the office who will be glad to offer whatever advice we can."

Like the boys, Miranda seemed to be forming a new circle of friends. Her coffee breaks and lunch hours were spent with Stevie and a couple of other working mothers, who patiently answered a dozen questions and offered valuable tips on schedule-juggling.

She was going to make this work, she finally concluded. It wasn't going to be easy, but if those other women could do it, so could she. And it wasn't as if she had any other choice—Lisa's letter had made it quite clear that the boys were Miranda's responsibility from now on. Lisa had completely abdicated all her parental rights, saying repeatedly that she believed Miranda would be a better parent to them than Lisa had ever been.

Miranda hoped fervently that Lisa was right. All she knew for sure was that she was going to do her best. She still didn't fully understand Lisa's choice, but she would deal with it. Somehow.

By the end of the week, Mark still hadn't called. Miranda suspected it hadn't been easy for him to restrain himself from checking on her and the boys. Maybe he thought she wanted him to stay away. After all, she had told him she needed time.

She'd thought he would call.

She knew she had hurt him when she'd pushed him away. But she hadn't thought he would give up quite so easily.

Saturday evening found her transferring pint-size blue jeans from the miniature washer to the equally-small dryer stacked above it in one corner of her kitchen. She noticed that the knees of several pairs of the jeans were getting rather worn; the boys would need new clothes for summer. Shorts and T-shirts and sandals. Then it would be time for school uniforms and backpacks and supplies.

She thought of the citrine-and-garnet ring she'd had her eye on, and she mentally kissed it goodbye. She could make do with the jewelry she had.

The twins were in the living room, playing with a couple of toys she had bought them last weekend. She heard them laughing and generally making a lot of noise—and then she heard a crash. It was followed, surprisingly, by voices raised in anger.

"It was *your* fault!"

"No, it was yours. I told you to be careful!"

"Now you broke it and—"

"I didn't break it, you did. Now we—"

"—and she's gonna be—"

"—and we're going to have to—"

"Boys!" Miranda broke in from the doorway, raising her own voice to be heard above them. They were squared off facing each other in the center of the room, their faces red, an inexpensive ceramic vase broken in three pieces on the floor beside them. "What's going on?"

Jamie inhaled sharply. "We're sorry, Aunt 'Randa. We didn't mean to break it. Don't be mad."

"You can sell our new toys to pay for it," Kasey offered anxiously.

"Can we still stay with you?" Jamie's question was barely loud enough for her to hear.

She sighed, feeling momentarily overwhelmed again. Was parenthood really a string of emotional landmines, always one step from lifelong trauma? She would have to ask her new support group at work Monday. She had a sneaky suspicion they would tell her it was exactly that.

"I am not mad at you, I'm not going to sell your toys, and I'm not going to send you away. Honestly, boys, get a grip, will you? It's just a vase. In the future, I would appreciate it if you would try not to break stuff, but it really isn't the end of the world."

Both boys blinked, processing what she had said, and the tone she had used. And then, Jamie said matter-of-factly, "I'll get the wastebasket."

"We'll be more careful, Aunt 'Randa," Kasey promised.

"Okay. Now, I've got to finish the laundry. So—chill, okay?"

Both looking more relaxed, the boys got busy cleaning up the first mess they had made while staying with her. She had a strong premonition that it wouldn't be the last.

Two weeks tomorrow. Mark stared glumly at the calendar on his desk late Friday afternoon, counting the days since Miranda had moved out of his house. Multiply that number by twenty or so, and it would add up to the number of times he had reached for the phone to call her, only to stop himself.

She had said she needed time. He had given it to her. He hadn't wanted to push her farther away by making a nuisance of himself—and okay, maybe he had hoped she would call him for help during that time. Had hoped she would realize that she needed him—to assist with the boys, if for no other reason. He was just pathetic enough to have welcomed even that.

Apparently she had been getting along just fine without him while he had been pining for her like a lovesick schoolboy.

"I'm gone for the weekend, Mark," Pam called from the other room. "'Bye, now."

She sounded awfully cheerful, practically on the verge of laughter. She must really be looking forward to the weekend, he thought enviously. "See you Monday, Pam. Lock the door behind you."

"Absolutely."

Maybe it was because his own mood was so bad that Pam's seemed unusually chipper. He really needed to snap out of this funk he had been in. Miranda wasn't coming back. She didn't want him in her life. Get over it.

Resting his cheek on his fist, he continued to stare at the calendar while he tried to talk himself into a better frame of mind. He didn't want to carry his bad mood into the evening with his daughters.

He heard footsteps in the doorway that led into the reception area. Because he didn't want Pam to see the misery that was probably still visible in his eyes, he didn't look up when he said, "I thought you were leaving."

"I did. I've come back."

He froze. That wasn't Pam's voice. Very slowly, he lifted his gaze.

Miranda leaned negligently against the doorjamb, her arms crossed in front of her, an easy smile on her face. She wore a bright yellow sundress that showed a lot of tanned skin, strappy sandals that revealed bronze-painted toenails and a gold toe-ring, and her usual flirty gold hoop earrings.

Golden girl, he thought with a catch in his throat. And damn, he had missed her.

"Pam let me in," she said while he was still trying to recover his wits sufficiently to form a coherent sentence.

"Where are the boys?"

"They're inside with Mrs. McSwaim and the girls. They seemed glad to see each other again."

Mark rose to his feet, still staring at her. "I'm sure they are. We—the girls have missed you guys. Um— how are the boys?"

"They're great. They like their day-care program. They were telling Payton all about it when I left them."

"And how are you?"

"Holding up," she said with a slight shrug. "Raising a couple of kids while working full-time isn't easy— but I didn't expect it to be."

His heart seemed to be beating in an odd rhythm. "Is there something I can do to help? Is that why you're here?"

"Actually, no," she said casually, stepping fully into his office and closing the door behind her. "I've been getting along just fine on my own—with a little advice from some working moms at the office. I didn't come here because I need anything from you, Mark. I came to assure you that I *don't* need your help."

The words hit him directly in the heart. He actually felt his shoulders sag in response. Resting one hand on his desktop, he said, "Well. Um. That's good, I guess. For you. That you're getting along so well, I mean."

But did she really have to grind his face in it?

His temper began to do a slow simmer. "So the only reason you came here was to tell me you don't need me?"

"No." She must have heard the irritation in his voice, but it didn't seem to concern her. She took a fluid step closer to him. "I never wanted to need you. I never wanted to need *anyone*. I've always believed I could handle anything that came my way—on my own. It's gratifying to find out for sure that I was right, even though I never imagined finding myself raising Lisa's kids."

"I had no doubt from the start that you could do it."

"I know." Her smile turned radiant. "You had more confidence in me than I did in myself."

She was confusing him to the point that his head was starting to hurt. "So you're here to...what? Thank me?"

"Not exactly." She stopped in front of him, her smile fading into a serious expression. "You said you didn't want a submissive companion. You said you were tired of being the one to do all the giving and get too little in return."

"I didn't say it quite that way," he countered, hope beginning to stir inside him again. "I said I want a partner, an equal. Someone who is quite capable of getting by on her own—but who chooses to be with me because she wants to, not because she has to."

"What a coincidence." Miranda rested her hands on his chest, and he could feel the tremors in her fingers even through the fabric of his buttoned-down white shirt. She wasn't quite as confident as she was pretending to be. "That's exactly why I'm here. Because I want to be."

He caught her hands in his. "Damn it, Miranda, you scared the hell out of me. I thought you were here to tell me it was over between us."

Her smile was tremulous now, her eyes glowing. "As far as I'm concerned, it's only just beginning. It was fear that kept me away from you for the first year I knew you, even when I was more drawn to you than to any man I'd ever met before. We both needed to be sure that it wasn't fear that brought me back to you. That's why I was so pleased to realize that I could get along without you. It just so happens that I don't want to."

His had his mouth on hers almost before she finished speaking.

Miranda locked her arms around Mark's neck, kissing him back with all the emotions she had tried to deny for the past year. She hadn't been entirely certain how he would greet her today. For all she had known, he might have come to the conclusion during the past couple of weeks that he was better off without her.

She was so very glad to know that he had missed her as badly as she had missed him.

It had finally occurred to her that, just as she had been waiting for him to contact her, he had probably been waiting for her to make the next move. For someone who had always been so bold about going after what she wanted, it had taken a surprising amount of courage for her to come here today. She hadn't regained her usual confidence until she had seen Mark sitting at his desk, looking so sad and lonely that her heart had twisted inside her.

He had been thinking about her. She was sure of it. And, for someone who had spent the past ten years avoiding emotional ties of all kinds, being wanted that badly was as daunting as it was heartwarming.

By the time he lifted his head, breaking off the explosive kiss, they were both gasping for air.

Mark lifted his hands to cup her face between them, searching her expression intently. "You're sure about this? You aren't going to change your mind?"

"Maybe it's taking you just a little longer to figure it out than it did me," she replied, her voice husky from emotion. "I'm not Lisa. And I'm not Brooke. When I make a commitment, I stick with it. I did it with my education. I've done it with my job. That's why I've avoided commitments I wasn't sure I could honor—because I never wanted to hurt anyone. Or be hurt, myself. But I've made a commitment to the twins, and I'm prepared to do the same with you. You asked me to give us a chance—and that's what I'm doing. I'm ready to find out where it will lead."

"And if it leads to the altar?" he asked, still watching her expression closely.

Perhaps he thought he would see panic there. Instead she smiled, if a bit shakily. "Then I'll honor that commitment, too. It does work out occasionally, you know. It has for your friend, Shane. And for his parents, who are about to celebrate twenty-five years of marriage. And even for my own parents, I guess, who are bound together by their own weird needs."

"You were afraid of feeling trapped. Suffocated. Tied down."

"All of which I *would* feel, in a situation that wasn't

of my choosing," she replied promptly. "I had no control over Lisa sending her boys to me, but I chose to keep them. And I've chosen to be with you."

His hands slid down to her shoulders, but he still looked worried. "After all your resistance, you aren't at all worried now?"

She suspected that there would have been a slightly hysterical edge to her laughter if she hadn't been able to contain it. "Are you kidding? I'm *terrified*. Four kids under six? A brand-new relationship with a man who's already thinking about the altar? I'm scared, but I'm not running. I'm still here—and still ready to give it my best shot."

"But what if—?"

"Mark," she interrupted with a sigh, clutching his shoulders. "I can't predict the future. Neither of us can. Do you think I could have predicted *this* a year ago? A month ago? All we can do is decide what we want and then try to make it work. Knowing it's going to be hard sometimes, knowing we'll make mistakes. Knowing the rewards are ultimately worth the sacrifices. Aren't those all things you've said to me during the past couple of weeks?"

"Yeah," he said after a moment. "I guess that's exactly what I've been trying to say."

She smiled. "Then shut up and kiss me again."

He obliged.

This kiss—and the next half dozen—ended with her sitting on his desk, her skirt tangled around her thighs, which were wrapped tightly around him. He had one hand on her breast, the other arm wrapped tightly around her, while she clung to him for dear life, one hand plunged into his thick, delightfully springy hair.

"If you only knew the fantasies I've had about you and me on this desk," she murmured into his ear, tracing the lobe with the tip of her tongue in illustration.

His laugh was rough. Sexy. Utterly masculine. "Maybe later we'll compare fantasies. I've got more than a few that involve you, as well."

"I can't wait." She kissed him lingeringly again, then reluctantly drew her mouth from his. "I suppose we had better go inside. Mrs. McSwaim could be wondering what's keeping us."

"I have a feeling Mrs. McSwaim knows exactly what's keeping us," he murmured, rotating his thumb to make her shudder in response. "She's a very perceptive woman."

"Still—"

He sighed and dropped his hand.

Helping her off the desk, he waited until both of them were somewhat collected before moving toward the door that led into his house. He turned to her before reaching for the doorknob. "We'll take this slowly," he promised. "We'll do it right. I won't rush you into anything you aren't ready for."

"Damn straight, you won't."

Her instantaneous reply made him laugh. "Right. I have fallen in love with a woman who definitely knows her own mind."

"And I'm in love with a man who is smart enough

to remember that in the future," she told him, patting his cheek.

As a declaration of their feelings, it was a rather prosaic moment, she thought as she followed him through the doorway. But as far as she was concerned, it was perfect.

Epilogue

Miranda spun into the hotel room, humming the tune to the last song they had danced to, her head still buzzing from champagne.

It had been an adults-only evening. And she had savored every moment of it. She was eagerly anticipating the rest of the night, she thought as she turned to her husband with a smile.

Smiling broadly, he caught her around the waist and twirled her into an impromptu dance. "Did you have a good time?"

She almost sang her reply. "I had a wonderful time."

"You're a little tipsy."

She laughed and looped her arms around his neck. "I'm drunk with love."

"Not to mention a couple of bottles of champagne," he said with a chuckle.

She reached up to kiss him. "You think we should call Mrs. McSwaim and check on the kids?"

"Mrs. McSwaim knows how to reach us if there's a problem," he replied firmly. "Tonight is for us. We only get a three-day honeymoon—we're going to make the most of every moment."

During the past eight weeks, they had learned to make the most of all their moments together. That was how long it had taken Miranda to realize that marriage was exactly what she wanted with him. She planned to make the most of every moment with him for the rest of her life.

The children had eagerly accepted the newest development in their eventful lives. There had been some turf battles, some concerns about the changes to come, but on the whole, they seemed pleased to be melding into a new family unit.

Miranda was under no illusions that all their problems were solved, and that the next few years would be easy ones. They had formed a blended family with four children who had been abandoned by their mothers, and with two adults who both carried baggage of their own. But she and Mark had agreed that burdens were much lighter when the weight was shared.

Holding her close, he gazed down into her eyes. "You haven't changed your mind?"

She didn't hesitate. "I haven't changed my mind."

"I'm sorry your parents weren't at the wedding."

At his urging to face her past, Miranda had called her parents. She had told them what was going on in her life, and asked them if they would be interested in getting to know her again. Instead they had expressed their disapproval that Lisa had borne children out of wedlock and then got herself into so much trouble that she couldn't be a mother to them. They had sanctimoniously condemned Miranda's decision to take those boys in, and to marry a man who was divorced and had children of his own.

She and Lisa had never listened to them when they had tried to "guide" them before, and look where it had gotten them, they said. The call had ended coolly, with them insincerely wishing Miranda luck and her telling them quite sincerely that she hoped they would enjoy the rest of their rigidly controlled lives.

"It was their loss," she told Mark with a shrug of resignation. She had reached out without expectations, so she hadn't been overly disappointed by the results. But in her mind, it was her parents who were missing out by not knowing their adorable grandsons.

As for Miranda, she considered herself immeasurably blessed to have Kasey and Jamie with her. When she looked back now at her former life—a string of empty parties and emptier friendships—she couldn't imagine going back. And now when she thought of her parents, she could do so with more pity than bitterness. So perhaps calling them had been the right thing to do, after all.

This, she thought, snuggling into Mark's arms, was where she belonged.

She tugged at the knot of his tie, ready to do away with the formality of clothing. "Since we only have three days…"

They had agreed it was all the time they could spare, between the need to spend time with the children and the demands of their jobs. They had already made arrangements to take a vacation as a family in October and attend the weekend anniversary party at the Walker ranch in Texas—a way for Mark to reconnect with *his* past.

Mark already had the zipper down on her dress, his hands slipping eagerly beneath the fabric. His lips moved against hers. "I love you, Miranda."

She shimmied out of the dress and offered herself to him wholeheartedly. "I love you, too."

They spent the rest of the evening throwing their own private little party. And Miranda planned for the rest of their lives to be a continuation of that celebration.

* * * * *

Be sure to read Gina Wilkins' next
FAMILY FOUND *romance*
from Silhouette Special Edition:
THE BORROWED RING.
Available November 2005.

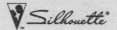

SPECIAL EDITION™

presents

the first book in a heartwarming new series by

Kristin Hardy

Because there's
no place like home
for the holidays…

WHERE THERE'S SMOKE

(November 2005, SE#1720)

Sloane Hillyard took a very personal interest in her work inventing fire safety equipment—after all, her firefighter brother had died in the line of duty. And when Boston fire captain Nick Trask signed up to test her inventions, things got even more personal… their mutual attraction set off alarms. But could Sloane trust her heart to a man who risked his life and limb day in and day out?

Available November 2005 at your favorite retail outlet.

Where love comes alive™

SPECIAL EDITION™

Don't miss the latest heartwarming tale from beloved author

ALLISON LEIGH!

A MONTANA HOMECOMING

(Special Edition #1718)
November 2005

Laurel Runyan hasn't been to Lucius, Montana, since the night her father supposedly murdered her mother—and she gave her innocence to Shane Golightly. Now, with her father's death, Laurel has come back to face her past...and Shane—a man she's never stopped loving....

Available at your favorite retail outlet.

Where love comes alive™

If you enjoyed what you just read,
then we've got an offer you can't resist!

Take 2 bestselling love stories FREE!

Plus get a FREE surprise gift!

COMING NEXT MONTH

SPECIAL EDITION